GUARDIANS OF THE GREAT
NORTH PACIFIC CASINO

GUARDIANS OF THE GREAT NORTH PACIFIC CASINO

Written and Illustrated by
Diana Tillion

VANTAGE PRESS
New York

Published by Vantage Press, Inc.
516 West 34th Street, New York, New York 10001

Manufactured in the United States of America
ISBN: 0-533-12853-6

Library of Congress Catalog Card No.: 98-90585

0 9 8 7 6 5 4 3 2 1

Foreword

One day in Seattle, September of 1989, I was having lunch with Clem Tillion, Harold Lokken, and Bob Thorstenson at the Canal Restaurant. They were getting together to discuss fisheries policies to be addressed at the next North Pacific Fishery Management Council meeting, and I, the listener.

The interesting thing about the fisheries is that on the surface there's a rather simple, almost romantic, aspect. Nothing could be further from the truth. It is one big gambling house with high stakes.

The men had greeted each other with pleasure based upon a long association and respect. I'm sure they didn't always agree (who does?) but knew their opinion came from the desire to serve the resources of the North Pacific. They sat down, ordered their preference from the menu, and looked out the window, hoping to see a sea lion in the waters of the canal before settling down to the issues at hand.

Clem smiled in a rueful manner. "As they say, 'We've met the enemy, and it is us.'"

Bob, always serious, replied, "It is frightening to know that the technology is there to fish out the entire North Pacific."

"Yes," Harold said, "it has happened so fast. We thought we had a handle on it. We did for a few years."

Completion of the North Pacific Railroad, in 1888, made it possible to ship products to the East from the West Coast. By 1895 fishermen in Gloucester, Massachusetts, complained of the competition created by West Coast fish coming into their markets. But as their stocks dwindled, a few of them sailed around the Horn to also enter the new fishing grounds—fishing grounds unbelievably rich.

Fishermen and boat builders flocked to Seattle from Scandinavia and from the Atlantic Coast to build the schooners that could, and would, brave the waters of the vast North Pacific as the fleet moved farther and farther northwest.

Harold Lokken's grandfather, John Strand, was one of these builders.

Harold Lokken, manager of the Fishing Vessel Owners Association in Seattle since 1924 (the association was formed in 1914) rubbed his head sadly in a gesture that could have been from a headache, or from confusion. "The tragedy," he declared, "is with the shortened sea-

sons and the increased capability of the fleet, the result is an inferior and more costly product to the consumer. We tried what was called The Grand Experiment in 1937 to pace the departure of the fleet, seeking to relieve the congestion for the outfitters, and to see if we could provide an even flow of fish to the market, thus avoiding the wide fluctuations in prices that occurred when there was a glut one week and a scarcity the next. It was not continued a second year. The fishermen preferred the chaos to waiting their turn to leave. Later we did form what was called The Halibut Production Control Board. Initially the board instituted a layup of seven days after each trip. It was possible to ask the fishermen to lay up after they had a load, versus asking them to wait to get to the grounds first. This layup was designed to improve the quality of the fish to the consumer, reduce the severity of the work to the fishermen, and give them increased prices by stretching out the landings. As it stood, a buyer could name his price when the market was glutted beyond bargaining. This control program lasted until 1977, except for a short period during World War II when the military controlled the fishing off the North Pacific, fearing dangers to the fleet. The program ended by 1977 because so many different types of fishermen had entered the fishery. There was no way to keep adequate control of it. Harold paused, seeing the waiter coming, sighed, and stated, "I think we should enjoy our lunch. I understand anxiety is bad for digestion."

They chuckled. "Good idea," they chorused.

Many efforts have been made to address these concerns: the Treaty of 1908 by scientists of the United States and Canada; the first Halibut Treaty in 1919, which led to the International Pacific Halibut Commission in 1924; the International North Pacific Fisheries Commission established in 1953; a commission comprised of members from Canada, the United States, and Japan. Each nation had four commissioners, a panel of advisors, and a scientific committee who determined species allocations while the commissioners and advisors divided the pie. This commission had no jurisdiction over the increasing number of foreign vessels in the Bering Sea and the Gulf of Alaska. Japanese, Russian, Taiwanese, Polish, South Korean, and other members created the Magnuson Act of 1976, establishing the 200-mile Fisheries Conservation Zone and, consequently, the nine management councils around the coast of the United States, of which the North Pacific Fishery Management Council serves the North Pacific.

The Alaskan salmon industry, which had been the largest fishing industry in the United States in the early 1900s, was not as fortunate in efforts of management in spite of the Act of 1906 and then the White Act of 1924, as well as others that were deftly lobbied down in Wash-

ington, D.C. by the cannery owners to a Congress willing to be obliging to their San Francisco countrymen to reap millions of dollars from the silver horde (as the salmon were aptly called) that swept up the coast of the territory of Alaska. Such a vast and remote place. The industry peaked in 1936 with 8.5 million metric tons of salmon harvested. In spite of late federal interest in conservation measures, the rapid decline in stocks was not reversed until Alaska gained statehood in 1958 and embraced fisheries management head on. The halibut and the salmon are the traditional fisheries, but there are others, each affecting the whole, with management becoming more and more complex.

The multipurpose of this book is to give a biographical sketch of a few men who have been involved and instrumental in changes in fisheries management in the North Pacific.

- Elmer Rasmuson, a banker
- Bob Thorstenson, a processor
- Harold Lokken, a representative of fishing vessel owners
- Clem Tillion, a politician
- Lee Alverson, a scientist
- Jim Branson, a bureaucrat
- Gordon Jensen, a halibut fisherman and public spokesman
- Brad Matsen, a journalist
- Tom Wardleigh, a pilot

Being privy to this scene as it unreeled has compelled me to speak of these gentlemen who have stayed the course with conviction of purpose to sustain a healthy fishery.

There is a section with each man's résumé, providing the full measure of his involvement, and also a section of data, starting in 1888 and continuing through to 1996, that tells the story of those hundred years. The first section of the book is in historical novel form (in a sense the spoonful of sugar . . .) into which biographical vignettes of these men are woven, plus a fictional main character whose role addresses some of the downside. The flashback sections are easily identified and are taken from personal interviews. The main characters meet on the Alaska Steamship *Aleutian* in 1947, traveling to Alaska—figuratively speaking "in the same boat" then, and in that same boat in 1996. The bad guy is not a real person.

The scene extends above the water and below, a world that even more acutely records the past and the present and predicts the future. Other players in the fisheries arena are here, too, as they act and interact in the sequence of events during the time frame I have chosen, 1947–1996.

The era, now, is the making of millionaires for a brief moment, and the cause of bankruptcy for those less prepared. A frantic element is growing. The North Pacific Fishery Management Council is struggling to address the need for limited entry in the face of almost overwhelming odds created by big money and narrow regional views. There is little romance of the sea. The stakes are high. No gold rush was ever ridden with greater enthusiasm, with more naked greed, clever and ruthless investors . . . and innocence. The fleet, no longer the pride of the Norwegian Americans, is viewed in simple context. This multinational industry is a heavy-stakes game. This new era is neither clumsy nor humorous, and, if not curtailed, will be (sadly) decimated, as have been many fisheries the world over. It has also been my observation that the men in fisheries are the most true of groups.

The fishermen, the field biologists, the scientists, the politicians, and the negotiators all believe in themselves and in their version of resource management, be it even the most rapacious or the most protectionist.

The battleground is visible and the players, real.

THEY CAME
BY SAIL.

THEY CAME
BY STEAM.

THEY CAME
BY DIESEL,

AND GASOLINE.

The Great North Pacific Casino
(Address—on the Sea. 130 W to 175 E,
/ 50 S to 65 N)

Diana Tillion

The North Pacific Casino
Resembles no gambling joint
You ever have seen. Be not deceived,
'Beats them all from Vegas to Boynt.

The ships are the chips costing dollars.
The cards or the dice are the fish.
The tables the market and weather,
Or the hand that matches the wish.

They come by the hundreds and thousands
To play for high stakes at a toss.
They know of many men's winnings,
And ignore those played at a loss.

A croupier is at every table
To monitor odds and for tricks,
They look like one of the players
As they move from table to mix

With the new fishermen that gather
Eyes shining with confident pride
That they have the magical number
And they're ripe for that wealthy sleigh ride.

GUARDIANS OF THE GREAT NORTH PACIFIC CASINO

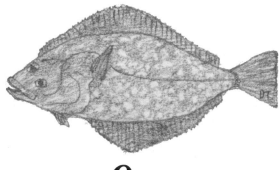

One

Visibility from the pilothouse of the huge, 400-foot "Fisher" was zero, save for a brief moment, now and again, between drenchings by the mountainous seas crashing over the bow of the huge factory ship. Captain Vincent and the factory foreman, Kim Cho, stood with their feet braced against the ship's lunging rhythm, as it pushed into the raging storm on the great Bering Sea. The wind slashed the tops off the twenty-foot swells, slamming tons of black-green water against the steel hull. The captain knew where they were. The wheelhouse was equipped with the finest radars, sonars, and every other electronic eye available in 1981.

The ship was a fish processor, built in the U.S.S.R. and operated by the Russians in joint venture with a Korean group, with smaller American catcher boats delivering the fish to be processed aboard this seagoing mother-ship. By law, the Soviet ship could process but not catch fish taken in waters under U.S. jurisdiction. The ship had a Russian captain, Captain Petrof, an old sea dog ready to retire. Petrof had been delighted when he discovered that the representative for the American fishing company providing the fishing fleet had sent a man who was also a certified captain. One who didn't mind spending time on the bridge and who was equally pleased that the Russian invited him to do so. The American had been reluctant to take the job. His own ship was in the yard, being overhauled. The company had been desperate for someone who would understand the whole process, and all but begged him to accommodate them.

The American catcher boats were three trawlers delivering to the factory ship. Transferring the "cod end" of the huge trawls, like giant

1

sausages, from one ship to the other, to be pulled over the stern, with thousands of pounds of fish which were then sorted. The desirable ones were processed and those too small or considered unmarketable, called bycatch, were dumped, as well as those fish that had a designated commercial quota and were to be sold only by so-licensed vessels.

"Thank the gods for the storm," Cho remarked. "The inspector can't come out here in this." Cho was an American-born Korean whose family was in the surimi fish paste business in Seoul. He had gone to his ancestral home to apprentice in the business and now supervised the making of the high-protein fish paste on this factory mother-ship. He was young and quick. Eager to please everyone. Eighty workers came under his directorship and the responsibility was intense, but no less heady, for such a young man. Captain Vincent, too, was young. Ten years of tugboating the North Pacific after maritime school gave him confidence. He had little in common with Cho, except that they were completely dependent upon the success of the other. According to the federal rules of the National Marine Fisheries Service at the end of the 1970s, every factory ship worked in U.S. waters was required to have an observer aboard. The observer had to be a marine biologist whose job was to log the contents of the huge tube-like net as it was dumped and sorted, isolating the product, as the target species was called, and bycatch, which represented all other contents that would be thrown overboard. The observer, a man or a woman, was a federal employee, not part of the ship's crew whose daily job was wet, cold, and intense, with the incentive that the harder they worked, the more money they made. This did not apply to the observer. The job of the observer, a woman, on this ship, looked like child's play to them as she moved around the sorting tables with pencil poised over her logbook, noting species, sizes, conditions, and numbers. There were a few women in the crew, but this one seemed different—too polite . . . too precise . . . too academic and earnest to be approachable. They did not socialize. Her name was Jean.

At the moment she was in her stateroom, sitting at a tiny desk with drawers that locked in place so the lurch of the ship could not spill the contents. Her logbooks were secured on a shelf above. She was intently writing, transferring figures from one book to another. A tiny calculator providing instant answers. The inspector was to arrive today. She smiled, happy for the reprieve the storm provided. By mid-afternoon the wind slacked off. The factory foreman ordered the nearest trawler to come alongside. The trawler, stabilized by the huge sack of fish off its stern, was steadier than the factory ship. Slowly it drew alongside. Captain Vincent pushed the button for the speaker system.

2

"Let the line," he ordered, and a crewman tossed a line off the stern of the factory ship, paying it out until it trailed far behind the stern. The trawler slipped slowly aft of the factory ship, carefully maneuvering to be able to pick up the trailing line. Tension, in spite of the hundreds of times the procedure was repeated, was intense.

"Secured the line!" the lineman yelled, as it was caught on the long gaff hook.

"Yo!" the captain answered in acknowledgment.

A crewman attached the line to the cod end of the trawl, tripped the lock, called the pelican release, and the huge tube of fish fell free of the trawler, to be pulled onto the stern of the factory ship. It was done. The huge factory ship steadied out as the full weight of the loaded net was pulled up the chute off the stern.

Books in order, Jean made her way aft, notepad held firmly, as she braced against the continuous surge of the vessel. She met the factory foreman as she stepped on deck. Cho bowed slightly, glancing to right and left but not really meeting her gaze. She nodded with barely a visible sign of recognition.

"No love lost there," one of the older men in the crew observed to his companion. To the crew, the observer was superfluous—maybe

3

even dangerous to their livelihood. She could force them to port for violating any one of a dozen rules about what they could catch and what they could not. Where they could fish or where not. To the factory foreman, she represented higher authority.

Handling the tons of fish went faster than seemed possible. Excess unwanted species were shoveled down a chute, provided for disposal, and the desired fish were pitched onto conveyor belts that took them below decks to the crew that gutted and cleaned them in preparation for the machine that turned them into the mixture that becomes surimi. Jean moved around, taking notes after examining each section.

"Hey! I hear a 'copter," someone yelled. "That inspector, I bet!"

"Jesus," another one said, tipping his head a little to one side to hear better, "that's a bureaucrat for you. Doesn't have the sense to know that this damn weather can kill him. He'll probably crash into us trying to land."

"Get moving," Captain Vincent yelled over the intercom. "Get that deck as clear as possible so the inspector doesn't fall and break his neck." Captain Petrof stepped into the pilothouse but remained silent.

The helicopter was suddenly overhead circling the plunging ship. Captain Vincent glanced at Petrof. The captain smiled and gestured that he was happy to watch.

On deck the crew scurried. The deck boss rushed around, giving orders to the crew to clear the central area. He seldom raised his voice, so they responded to that urgency well. Cho moved around the perimeter. When things looked like they were well in hand, he bolted for the companionway leading to all quarters and to the pilothouse above.

The helicopter settled slowly down toward the tiny helipad on top of the ship. The pilot gauged the action of the vessel to know just when to drop his skids to the wildly tilting platform. Captain Vincent watched, radio in one hand, and jog stick, to steer the ship, in the other. He'd taken control of the ship from the first mate in this critical circumstance. He sent the mate to tend the locking straps for the helicopter upon touchdown. "Take three men with you to assist," he ordered, anxiety sharpening his voice. To the captain, the need to have the ship safe for these landlubbers unfamiliar with the sea and to watch a landing that could turn instantly into a disaster caused more stress than could any weather the ship might encounter. At the moment of this most intense concentration, Cho walked into the pilothouse and rushed to the window to watch the helicopter's approach.

"What the hell are you doing here?" the captain shouted at him. "Get down there and keep the crew going." His head spun around when the sound of the helicopter engine changed from a steady howl to a warbling, shrill, insistent whine. "On second thought, get up there, and help tie down. . . . Go," he shouted when the young man hesitated. Captain Petrof laughed softly. He obviously enjoyed the chaos.

As the ship hit the bottom of the swell and started up the advancing one, the helicopter moved forward, over the heliport, and the ship rose to meet the pontoons. They had landed. It was instant.

The first mate, the factory foreman, the radio operator, and the cook (who had appeared at the pilothouse door at the critical moment to ask if anyone wanted coffee) all reached forward to slap the holding straps around the pontoons and lock them in place. Hardly more than a minute had elapsed from touchdown to security.

"Mother Mary, save me from this crazy job!" the cook groaned as he hung on to the strap that secured his corner of the aircraft.

The chopper's rotors slowly wound down in the stiff wind, the door opened, and the flapping oilskins of the inspector appeared as he awkwardly backed out, clinging to the door frame. The first mate stood by to grab him if necessary. Inside the helicopter, the pilot was laughing, slightly hysterical, "It's damn sure true. You are incredible. I'd never have tried that. You son-of-a-gun, you scared the hell out of me."

Tom Wardleigh smiled. "It was all in a day's work in the old days," he said modestly. "I'm going aboard to say hi to the Captain. You, being the pilot, have to stay here and baby-sit this roller coaster." He easily climbed out, placing his feet to accommodate the familiar unsteady surface.

In the pilothouse, Inspector Lujak was logging in. He watched the mate write down his arrival time and the purpose of his visit. He was

glad for the pause before going on deck, hoping he'd stop shaking by then.

When Tom Wardleigh entered the pilothouse, Captain Vincent gave a shout of joy. "Tom! Good grief! I should have realized it might be you. All the crazy stories my dad tells about the old days. Didn't know you flew helicopters." He extended his hand warmly.

Tom Wardleigh grinned. "Well, shucks, I wasn't the pilot; he's up there getting seasick," he said, pointing toward the heliport. "They said in the Anchorage control room the guy was supposed to come out here, and figured they'd cancel because of the storm. I knew you were in charge of this critter, so I just thought I'd come along and show Larry a few old Grumman Goose tricks. Nothing to it; matter of timing," he said casually. "How're your folks? Haven't seen them in a long time."

Captain Petrof, the inspector, and Cho left the pilothouse and the personal conversation of the captain and the pilot to move down the multitude of stairs and companionways to the work deck aft.

Turning a sharp corner, they ran smack into one of the crew, oilskins and gloves still wet and slimy.

"Oh, my God, my God . . . Come fast . . . Jean . . . the observer . . . I think she's dead. She looks really dead as can be. Oh, my God, my God," the crewman kept repeating in quieter and quieter tones until he was mumbling, rocking forward and back in agony.

6

They pushed past him and ran to the work area.

Fish were everywhere, slowly shifting with the surge of the ship, forgotten by the stunned crew who surrounded the huge bin behind which the body had fallen. A two foot space, allowing access to the back of the bin, exactly accommodated the body of the girl.

The inspector pushed through the crowd. Reaching the bin and seeing the girls boots from that end, he made his way to the other end. He dropped to his knees and placed his fingertips at her throat to determine if she was still alive. He drew back, shaking his head. He searched the faces of the silent mob. "How did this happen?" he asked.

They shook their heads, as if pulled by one string, back and forth. "I don't know. We don't know," the deck foreman stammered. "We were all so busy." They all nodded in agreement.

"Well, damn it, one of you must have seen it happen!"

They all shook their heads again. They backed away. The inspector kneeled down and carefully pulled the girl's body from behind the huge bin. He checked her over for any major injury. Slowly standing up, he shook his head. His distress mirrored on his face. He indicated to two large men to find a plastic bag for the body and to take it to the heliport and load it in the plane. He would take it back to Anchorage.

His face set in the impassive expression of an inspector. Turning to the crowd, he asked again, "How did this happen?"

Every face was blank. "We were so busy hurrying to clear the deck for . . . for your arrival. I guess she just fell and we didn't see it," a middle-aged man said. "It's a pretty noisy place here when we're haul-

ing the trawl." The inspector looked questionably from one face to another. A few members of the crew spoke English, but the majority spoke either Russian or Korean. They shook their heads.

The inspector pulled the notebook out from under the body. "Where are her other records?" he asked the factory foreman, who stood, face in his hands, blocking the sight of the body. Cho looked up, face flushed with emotion. "In her stateroom," he said.

"Who has access?" the inspector asked.

"I guess the steward, or whoever cleans her room, but first we have to inform the captain. He has to order access. No one can do anything like that without his okay," Cho said, recovering a semblance of composure. Captain Petrof, standing in a circle of workers, appeared quite angry. His red face and posture was that of a furious man. Those around him were gesturing wildly, shakingly protesting. "I think I'd wait a minute," the foreman advised. He held out his hand and pointed to a young man standing to one side. "There's the steward," he said, beckoning to the young man to come forward. He explained their need to have access to the stateroom. The steward walked quickly across the deck to Captain Petrof. The captain gave a curt nod to the young man and continued his flood of statements to the workers.

The inspector stepped closer to the group surrounding Captain Petrof, hoping to hear some word of English to understand the tirade at a crew obviously already shattered by the event of the girl's death. He shook his head in frustration. Turning to the steward, he asked, "Why is the captain so angry? Why is he speaking Russian? Is he accusing someone of foul play? Is there a reason on this ship to suspect foul play?"

The steward shook his head. "No," he said, "and the captain always speaks in Russian when he is angry or excited. And to answer your question, there is nothing on this ship that would warrant anyone's death." His expression was that of tightly held emotion.

The inspector stared at him, as if to discover some deceit in his expression, then nodded curtly and asked, "Where is her stateroom?"

The steward turned to walk down the companionway to the girl's quarters.

Tom Wardleigh had excused himself from the pilothouse to follow the men to the deck. He'd watched the actions of the inspector and the expressions of the crew, and studied the anger of Captain Petrof, wondering at the vehemence. He followed the young man, not wanting to miss any part of this event. The steward was a pleasant young man, fair of complexion and athletic in build. "She was so nice," he said. "So nice," he kept repeating, as he led them to the room and unlocked the door. His slight accent suggested he was foreign. "German?" Tom asked casually. "Nyet; Russian," was the instant reply. "My grandfather," he added hastily. Tom smiled ruefully. He knew that's what they all say when they try to slip into the United States.

The inspector sat at the tiny desk not long before occupied by Jean. He carefully examined the files. "Everything is in excellent order," Inspector Lujak said, as he gathered all the material from the desk and drawers, placing them in a cardboard box someone had thoughtfully provided.

Tom, wandering about the room unnoticed, retrieved a wad of paper from the back edge of the top bunk. He stepped into the companionway and unfolded it.

"I can't bear it any longer. I must stop," was written on it. *Hmm, was this a boyfriend? Or perhaps the job?* he wondered. He folded the piece of paper and put it in his pocket.

The inspector and Tom made their way to the heliport, where Tom instructed the four men, who had struggled with the wrapped body of the girl, up to the heliport and into the freight area of the aircraft. He advised the men who were to release the helicopter to wait until they heard the engines reach full power, then to release the straps. "The timing is critical; there will be some power and then full throttle. You will be able to tell. Be sure to have a good grip on those straps yourself," he said, as he pulled himself into the aircraft.

When the aircraft door was locked the pilot turned to Tom. "Now, let's see you get us off this roller coaster."

Tom remained passive for several upsurges and downthrusts of the ship as it breasted the huge waves. Then, turning to the pilot he said, "Now, rev up a little on the down in preparation to give it all it's got at the crest of the wave to leave the heliport as the ship drops off the next swell." The pilot gave it half power, and looked nervously out at the men manning the straps. He gave it full throttle when the ship reached the top of the swell. The men let go of the straps; the helicopter literally seemed to be tossed off the top of the ship, and they were airborne.

Tom turned to the pilot. "Report to Anchorage now. There has to be an investigation. I assume the Coast Guard will handle the transportation," he advised. The pilot reached for the mike and relayed the information. He hung up the mike and grinned at Tom.

"They won't have your help to land on that helipad."

"No problem," Tom assured him. "The Coast Guard Airwing is the finest. They do it all the time."

Putting his hand in his pocket, Tom felt the small piece of paper. Taking it out of his pocket, he was surprised to see "R. Oblensky" written on the outside. He'd missed that.

In Anchorage the next day, the papers shouted the news:

10

OBSERVER DIES ABOARD FACTORY SHIP

The headlines jumped out like a fire alarm to the three members of the North Pacific Fishery Management Council. Jim Branson, the executive director, had ordered the paper for those members he knew would gather for breakfast at the hotel where the council was meeting.

Clem Tillion scanned the column to determine the cause. He set the paper aside. "Looks like a fairly common accident," he said. He shifted position, a gesture of tension that belied his casual remark.

Lee Alverson had picked up the paper. He read the extensive article carefully. Harold Lokken walked into the room, paper rolled under his arm. Harold spotted them all in the dining area and stepped quickly forward to join them, nodding to Clem and Jim. Lee did not look up; he'd turned to the second page, and was seemingly buried in folds of paper.

"Is it bad?" Clem asked, sorry now that he hadn't read it all.

Harold's expression was thoughtful. "The accident seems the usual to-be-expected type of thing—falling, you know. But there's something about it, a gut feeling, that seems off," he replied. "And because it is an observer, they will use that to further object to the observer program, I'm sure."

"Good God," Jim snorted, "accidents happen every day out there. It's a dangerous business." He paused. "We may have to provide a better training program for them," he said thoughtfully.

"They shouldn't take the job if they don't want the risk," Clem stated flatly, his politically wise brain knowing the endlessness of protectionist intervention beyond basic rules. "Thank goodness it isn't for the council to address." Seeing more of their group arriving, he waved to Oscar Dyson and Bob Thorstenson as they walked into the dining area to join the others.

Lee Alverson gasped, "Good grief; listen to this: 'The storm that would have canceled any other pilot was made possible by the assistance of an old Fish and Wildlife flier, Tom Wardleigh, who went along for the ride.'"

They all burst out laughing, recalling thirty years of hair-raising tales of Tom Wardleigh's impeccable, if scary, skill as a pilot.

"That's too much; I thought he was retired long since," Oscar said.

Unknown to them at that moment, upstairs, the council (North Pacific Fisheries Management Council) secretary was accepting testimony time for a Mr. Oblensky, to address the issue of observers.

Clem leaned back, pulling on the chain of his pocket watch. He studied the timepiece for a moment, then stood up. "Time to start," he said. He was the chairman of the North Pacific Fishery Management Council, having followed in Elmer Rasmuson's, and then Harold Lokken's footsteps.

The room was abuzz with the news. Speculation was rampant on whether there had been foul play. Had there been the proper investigation? "Women shouldn't be allowed to be observers, anyway," one particularly loud voice stated. "That's been nothing but a headache."

Chairman Tillion stared at the agitated man. His eyes gave an intense stare that made the man draw back and look from side to side, as if the stare were a physical thrust to avoid. Clem turned toward those sitting in the room, his expression softening, and assured the crowd that a thorough investigation was taking place concerning the matter. "There is nothing to do but wait for the results of the inquiry, and to get down to the agenda and think about the subjects before us," he said. "I know the news is shocking, but had it not been an observer, or a girl, it would hardly be noticed. Risk is part of the scene. You would be shocked by the statistics. Many of us here have witnessed the growth of this industry. Its very nature is wrought with pain and heartbreak, and yet it is so vital, so personally compelling, and so important to the whole world." He paused, then added in a softer tone, "I well recall when winter king crab fishing started in lower Cook Inlet. Eleven fishermen were drowned from the little village of Seldovia."

Oscar Dyson nodded his confirmation of that statement.

Clem looked at Oscar. "There's a man who could really elaborate on the dangers of fishing, as each of you can if you are well informed."

Members of the North Pacific Fishery Management Council at the crescent-shaped table in the front of the room looked at each other and grinned a wry grin. They faced a large audience of men and women representing every aspect of the fishing industry.

The room was silent as the secretary quietly distributed scientific data reports to the council members.

They, in that quiet moment, remembered that beginning time.

The chairman was remembering, also. Having focused on Oscar, and that bitter winter, triggered the whole scene of how it was thirty-four years ago, coming to Alaska, and the subsequent entry into fishing.

Thirty-four years before, in the spring of 1947, Clem Tillion was making his way toward the big Alaska Steamship, SS *Aleutian,* at the pier in Seattle. He was early and had chosen to hike along the waterfront before having to board the ship, his thin frame looking taller than it was, topped by bright red hair and a military crew cut. A duffel bag rested against his leg, dropped in haste, when he spotted a halibut schooner tied along the pilings below. Coming from Long Island, he recognized the New England ship for what she was—one of those that had come around the Horn from the North Atlantic to fish the North Pacific. The ship was the epitome of the romance of the sea.

He envied those crew members he could see moving about the deck attending the patterned activity of the vessel.

Turning to the stranger approaching him, Clem asked eagerly, "Is it hard to get a job on one of those schooners?" nodding toward the ship below.

The man stopped. He wore bib overalls and looked more like part of the crew that would tend to the needs of the pier than a fisherman.

"You a Norwegian?" the burly man asked.

"No," the young man replied, his voice breaking at the end of that single syllable, revealing the youth he was trying to disguise.

"I've been watching fishermen for a long time, for years and years, being more or less conscious of the cost of things. Been on both sides of the scale." The stranger laughed self-consciously, "Tried it once, you know. I can honestly say that I think a fisherman would pay to go fishing. Nothing else explains how reckless they are with money. Some call it the romance of the sea, but there's a goodly portion of greed involved, too." He shifted his position. "Of course, the Norskies are the halibut fleet; that's what they're called; mostly Norwegian, they are. They're

13

the top of the line when it comes to fishermen. They came around the Horn heading for the North Pacific. Oh, there were some other fellows like Newfoundlanders and Nova Scotians . . . but those Norwegians really topped the list. The interesting thing about fishermen is they never talk about the guy who doesn't make it. Those schooner crews live offshore. They are a separate breed of cat. There's no dirt under their fingernails. Just a little blood and scales. You wonder what they talked about when they came ashore that their wives and kids could understand. Plenty, I guess, 'cause the boys followed in their fathers' footsteps. Couldn't wait to follow."

The older man paused, his expression softening, remembering how it was to be so young and eager. "No chance, son. You gotta be Norwegian." He looked into the sharp blue eyes. The mouth curled at the corners in a humorous way; the body, the human equivalent of a coiled spring ready to shoot off in the desired direction. "So, you wanna be a fisherman. Where you headed?" he asked, looking down at the duffel bag.

"To Alaska. Steerage, on Alaska Steam," was the enthusiastic reply.

"You a fisherman back east?" the older man asked.

The young man hesitated, longing to say that he was. "I spent some time on my uncle's boat," he qualified. "And I fished for the mess hall in the South Pacific," he added.

The man stared at him. "You're too young to have gone to war."

Clem straightened up to be as tall as possible. "I enlisted when I was seventeen. In the CBs. Was sent to Tulagi in the South Pacific."

The man shook his head.

Clem's grandfather, his father, and his uncle were architects in New York City. He was bolting that city-boy image, admiring the heroes of the West, the courage of the high seas, and the glory of war.

"You should have stayed back east with your uncle, kid; they're all Norskies out here," the man said again, and continued on down the pier.

Clem would carry that moment with him to Alaska, knowing that the halibut schooner and many others like it traveled parallel to the steamship he was boarding.

Prior to World War II, the sea was the only access to Alaska. There were small freight boats that traversed the Inland Passage of Southeast Alaska and a very few that crossed the gulf to the Aleutian Islands. The journey on Alaska Steam was transportation, to be sure, but it also carried a touch of the vacation mood about it, at least for those passengers with staterooms. Far below decks, the steerage passengers would be bunched together for a cheap but unglamourous journey.

The 400-foot hull of the SS *Aleutian* loomed over the pier like a monstrous black wall. Lines from the giant booms hauled cargo up and over the side, to disappear into the vast hold of the ship. Groups of people huddled together, talking in low tones of private conversation, or stood in loosely energetic masses. Single figures stood around, isolated in the crowd.

Clem wasn't sure what the protocol was for steerage passengers so he stood a little to one side watching the activity. When the gangway was lowered for boarding, he made no move to get in the line that immediately formed to go aboard, eager to give their tickets to the purser at the top of the ramp.

Once on the deck many scurried inside, but others made their way along the rail to stand above their friends or families below, in order to wave and shout last-minute messages of farewell.

Clem was startled when a large group of Filipinos appeared behind him; he waited for the last heavily laden passenger to stagger up the ramp before following with quick and agile steps.

At the approach of one of the Filipinos, who looked at him and smiled, Clem returned the greeting and asked, "Steerage?"

The Filipino nodded yes, so Clem, tossing his duffel bag onto his shoulder, followed.

The steerage area was a large open space that could have been a cargo hold. Racks of bunk beds, five high, and a place to attach holding bins for personal gear were the very un-private quarters.

The Filipinos were obviously familiar with the routine, as they immediately located a bunk and quickly stowed their personal things. They completely ignored Clem as though he weren't there. He continued down the length of the room, seeing a place where he could tuck himself into a corner. Approaching it, he tossed his duffel bag easily onto the top bunk and climbed up, using the lower bunks as a ladder. On top, he sat down, and, looking around, was startled to see another young man like himself on the opposite top bunk.

"Where did you come from?" he asked. " I didn't see you on the dock."

The fellow lowered the book he was reading and looked at Clem. His expression, noncommittal. "I slipped onboard earlier, knew one of the crew, knew it would be a zoo," he said, nodding toward the chattering Filipinos. He raised the book, shutting out the figure of his new companion, in a gesture that clearly said the conversation was over.

Clem was not to be put off. "This is just like a troop ship. Well, not exactly; the linen looks fresher." He laughed, "A lot fresher, although it's not as crowded. Oh, well, maybe it isn't like a troop ship, after all," he said. "Say, what's the deal with all the Filipinos?" he asked as he arranged the things from his duffel bag in the storage bin. "How fast is this tub?" he asked. "Where are you going?" he added, not waiting for an answer. "I'm going to Seward," he volunteered. "My name is Clem Tillion."

The young man lowered the book far enough to peer over at his energetic companion. His expression, unchanged. "My name is Jim Branson, the Filipinos work in the canneries, and you talk too much," he stated bluntly and settled back with his book, once again blocking any possible exchange.

Clem stared at the back of the book. The guy did tell his name, so he couldn't be too antisocial. He started to say something else but decided not to press his luck. He put the rest of his gear away and tried to stretch out on the bunk, but the excitement of what he was embarking on catapulted him upright and off to investigate what there was to see.

Jim lowered the book far enough to watch the skinny figure fly through the air, hardly pausing when it landed and setting off down

the length of the room, deftly dodging any of the Filipinos in the way. He was tempted to follow but forced himself to stay in the bunk until the ship started to move away from the pier.

Clem made his way up the narrow stairs to the lower deck, noting the sign that warned steerage passengers that they were confined to "this deck level, and below, only." He strolled around the deck. There were stragglers on the dock still waving good-bye. He walked around to the outer side of the ship and looked across the water at other port facilities and ships, thinking of the halibut schooner he had seen earlier. How grand it would be to stand on that deck and look at this scene!

The sound of the ship's whistle, announcing its departure in fifteen minutes, was a familiar and homey sound. Clem smiled as he walked along the rail. At the door to the corridor, he went in and turned up the wider stairs to the upper deck. Outside he walked slowly along the rail, leaning out to wave every so often and keeping a watchful eye out for a steward or the ship's personnel that might spot him as a steerage passenger. Soon the lines were loosed and the big ship began to slowly move in reverse, then forward, away from the pier. The journey had begun.

Like bees in a hive, the passengers scurried around locating their staterooms, the lavatories, the dinning hall, and the lounge. The majority of them were involved with the fishing industry, migrating north for the summer's season, like the Filipinos below. There were groups of folks who knew each other, happy to be back again on the ship, making new acquaintances, meeting old and for a brief respite from work. Other passengers included many ex-servicemen, like Clem, heading north. Some of them had been stationed in Alaska while others were restless to see the last frontier. There were wives and children of other servicemen who had asked to be discharged in the territory when their hitch was up because they had succumbed to the spell of the country. The war was still fresh in everyone's mind. The sense of victory, a pervasive energy as positive as sunshine.

There were miners heading north to the interior where the war had not closed the mines. There were passengers returning home from business trips or family visits. Harold and Alice Lokken were a rare pair onboard. Harold was taking Alice up the coast of Southeast Alaska to see the fishing ports that she had heard about for the past twenty years. They would disembark at Juneau, not crossing the gulf to Seward, to catch the ship on its way south. Harold was the manager of the Fishing Vessel Owner's Association of Seattle and intimately knew the industry. Harold and Alice enjoyed first-class accommodations, as did Elmer Rasmuson, who was a banker from Anchorage.

The lounge was the gathering place for all passengers except those from steerage. It was well equipped with a small bar and comfortable chairs for those who wished to sit and read or visit. Slot machines added a bit of excitement for those of that inclination. A small dance floor promised an evening of pleasure. Music was provided by the adjacent jukebox or there was the possibility of live music. Its chummy, overstuffed atmosphere, low ceiling, and dim lights were inviting and visually comforting.

The seating in the dining hall was designated. Passengers were assigned a table number and a chair. Meals were served in two sittings, and that was indicated as well. First or second.

The captain's table was the largest in the room. The captain was always seated at the first sitting. It was his prerogative to choose from the passenger list who would share his table for that social hour. The other senior officers shared the table with appointed guests in the second sitting.

The steerage passengers were served in a mess hall below. It was a cafeteria-style dining room with long tables.

The ship was immaculately clean and the crew professional in manner.

The late afternoon sun slanted through the haze that hovered over Puget Sound, softening the contours of the islands, adding a dreamlike quality to the floating ship—as if it were not an object of thousands

of tons carefully calculated not to sink, but a leaf drifting between the islands, through Puget Sound, up the Strait of Georgia, past Vancouver Island, into Queen Charlotte Strait, then north-northwest into Queen Charlotte Sound.

Clem was startled by the dinner chimes as he stood on the deck watching the passing scene. A simple melody played on a five-bar xylophone in the hands of a waiter walking down and around the deck. The first call to dinner.

Clem waited until the messenger had gone around the stern of the ship then dashed inside, and down the stairs to find the dining room below. It was easily located by the traffic and the fragrance of food. He was hungry.

Jim was standing there with a tray. The line inched along. Clem was two men behind him. They exchanged nods of recognition. Tray loaded, Jim chose a place to sit and moved over a little to indicate room for Clem, who had decided he wouldn't talk at all unless asked. But Clem couldn't refrain from remarking, "Never heard where you were headed."

"I'm getting off at Wrangell. Got a job with the Fish and Wildlife Service running a patrol boat," Jim said.

"You must have been running boats before."

"Yeah, fishing off the West Coast. Puget Sound to Santa Barbara, trolling," Jim added.

"You must have seen some nasty weather on that open coast," Clem exclaimed, impressed.

"These inland waters won't be anything compared to that," Jim said. "Need a few more charts, of course."

"Like a cigarette?" Jim asked, when they had finished eating.

"Nope; never started. Costs too much," Clem said.

"Well, I'm going out on deck and have a smoke," Jim stated, and stood up to leave, picking up the now foodless tray to deliver to the designated place.

"I'll join you. It's really fine out there," Clem said, pleased to have the silence broken.

In the dining room Elmer Rasmuson sat at the captain's table. He always sat at the captain's table. He'd traveled on Alaska Steam many times and was on a first-name basis with all of the officers.

Elmer was a medium-sized man. A neatly trimmed mustache gave a debonair touch to his expensive, but tasteful, attire topped by dark hair and gray-blue eyes. His expression was intense, yet polite, not missing any detail of what was going on around him. One could sense that he was a decisive businessman. He looked like the banker that he was.

Elmer was happy to be on the ship with old friends. "After we know what we're ordering, a bottle of your best wine for the table," he said to the waiter. Then, looking around, he added, "Make it two." He smiled at the captain. "Always good to be onboard," he said. The captain grinned.

"I suppose you may have some exciting new stories of flying into the bush and hunting the wild game or fishing the rushing streams?" the captain said lightly, but with a tinge of envy in his voice.

Elmer laughed, pleased for the acknowledged recall of past conversations.

At the far end of the table, Alice Lokken leaned toward Harold and whispered, "Who is that? Is he from the East?"

Harold studied Elmer with blank, hooded eyes. "Could be, but he seems to know too many people. If he lived in Seattle, I would know him, so he must live in Alaska."

Harold Lokken, as manager of the Fishing Vessel Owners Association in Seattle, not only knew the fishermen and their vessels, but also knew all the businessmen they dealt with. No one in Seattle in the business world was unfamiliar to him. Alice was a petite young lady, fair and vivacious. Harold's inscrutable stillness was in direct contrast. His attentiveness to her revealed a thinly veiled romantic alliance.

"His clothes are definitely from New York or Boston," she whispered.

"Decide what you want to order Alice, and then we'll find out," Harold advised, putting first things first.

While Elmer carefully decided what the wine would be at the captain's table, three very hungry young men paced the deck, waiting for the second seating in the dining hall. Young Bob Thorstenson, at six-

teen, thought he might starve to death and wished he had somehow been able to be placed with the first sitting. He'd ask his uncle how to do that when he got to Juneau for the return to his home at Point Roberts. Lee Alverson had missed lunch. He'd had too many details to take care of for the trip. He was going to Juneau to organize the summer stream surveys at the Federal Fish and Wildlife Station. Tom Wardleigh was also traveling to Juneau. He was a pilot and was to fly a plane back to Seattle.

"I'm perishing. How about you?" Lee asked as Bob passed him for the third time. Bob grinned and rolled his eyes, his cheeks flushing with the knowledge that his hunger was so obvious. "Man, I could eat a horse," he replied. Tom unobtrusively moved a little closer to listen in. He stood with his head slightly inclined. His tall, thin frame draped against the rail. An amused expression animated his otherwise passive posture.

"Where are you going?" Lee asked, making conversation.

"To Juneau to visit my uncle. I made enough money in the cannery for this trip," Bob said proudly.

"What cannery?"

"Salmon and clams at Point Roberts. I guess we'll be going past it in the dark," Bob said, his handsome face brightening, thinking of it, while his voice expressed his regret that he could not point it out to them.

"Is that home?" Lee asked.

"Yes. My grandparents emigrated there from Canada. They wanted to fish. My grandmother worked all winter tying a net. They did well the first year, but the next year was a failure so they bought a farm. I'm a farm kid, but I started working in the cannery when I was twelve."

Lee slapped him on the shoulder. "Sounds good to me," he said. "I'm a school boy myself. Fisheries," he added.

Bob stared at him. "You mean college, I guess."

"Yes," Lee confirmed.

"I guess you'll be a 'fish hawk' someday. Maybe you are now," Bob said, looking at Lee with a certain reserve.

"Looks like you don't care for the enforcement side of fisheries," Lee observed. "No; I'm in the science end of it."

"You're a scientist?" Bob asked. "You seem so . . . ah . . . normal. I mean, you know, regular."

Lee laughed. "Well, you know, Bob, I don't consider myself a full-fledged scientist yet, but I hope to be one. And yes, I am 'just a regular guy.' You'll find that that's what we all are. One regular guy does one thing and another does something else. Not too many want to do the tedious work of being in the sciences."

Tom hadn't said a word. He stood beside them as they all leaned against the rail, looking at the scene sliding past. Silent now in their own thoughts; hunger, for a moment was forgotten.

"What do you do?" Bob asked, leaning over to look at Tom.

"I'm a pilot. I fly airplanes for fun and profit," Tom replied with a grin so infectious that Bob smiled.

"Boy, that sounds like fun." Bob looked from one man to the other. "Man," he said, "a scientist and an airplane pilot!" Both young men laughed. They suddenly felt much older. It felt good.

Inside, the captain's table had become genial, indeed.

"Yes, I have been from the East, but only because I went to Harvard and spent some time in New York. I'm an Alaskan," Elmer Rasmuson had replied to Harold Lokken's question. "My mother came to Yakutat in 1901 as a missionary for the Swedish Covenant Church, and my father came three years later to teach school and also to work at the mission. I was born there in 1909. We left Yakutat in 1914. We went to Minneapolis for a year but then returned to Alaska, where my father passed the bar exam in Juneau. In 1916 we went to Skagway, where I grew up." He smiled. "I learned Tlingit, Swedish, and English

22

right along with learning to walk. It was a bit confusing." He chuckled, but his expression was rueful.

"Yes, cross-cultural kids have a tough go, but I dare say it has been an advantage, too," Harold observed.

"Why would you live in Alaska if you've gone to Harvard and lived in New York?" Alice asked.

"My father brought me back to help in his bank, and I've stayed," Elmer answered.

"The bank at Cordova?" Harold guessed, his attention sharpened.

"Well, yes. Obviously you know something of the story. The fellow was really trying to keep his cannery going and that's why he absconded with the money. Of course he unwisely couldn't see that it cost more to can the fish than he could sell it for, so he opted to take his life than face the world. The worst thing was he destroyed the records, so it was a terrible job to square it around. My father straightened it out with his own money, then let the other Cordova bank take it over." He paused, shaking his head sadly. "It nearly broke him." He paused, then added, "In every way. The fishing industry is such a gamble."

"I guess your father was the first banker in Alaska."

"Oh, no. A man named Harrison in Juneau was. He failed, but B.

23

M. Behrends took it over. He's really the first. The Canadian Bank of Commerce, which served all of the gold trail, was the first bank. It closed in 1910 because of the decline in business," Elmer said.

"After the panic of 1907," Harold reasoned.

Elmer nodded, then laughed. "In a lighter vein, that bank was the scene of a most bizarre holdup. On September 15, 1902, a man walked into the bank holding a revolver in one hand and a stick of dynamite in the other. He demanded twenty thousand dollars. The employees behind the counter ducked out of sight. The man fired three warning shots to impress them of the seriousness of his request. The concussion from the shots set off the dynamite and he was blown to bits. He was the only casualty. Of course, the building had to be repaired."

"Wonderful story," Harold roared through the burst of laughter.

After the laughter subsided, Elmer continued, "Our bank, the Bank of Alaska, opened in that building on March 18, 1916. The bank now is the National Bank of Alaska." Turning to Harold, he asked, "What is your business?"

"I'm with the Seattle Fishing Vessel Owners Association, an organization of vessel owners who meet to discuss problems with the industry and with the halibut crews. We try to bring some sense of order to the fleet and to the marketplace. No small chore, dealing with independent fishermen, and demanding markets."

"So, this is just for the halibut fishery? Is the fleet of so much consequence?" Elmer asked, surprised.

Harold smiled, straightening up in his chair a little, pride in the fleet evident in his expression. "Well, the first load of halibut to go out East left Puget Sound in 1888 on the newly constructed railroad. The fleet has continued to increase."

Elmer was impressed. "Really. I was aware of the salmon industry in Alaska—the trap fishery, you know. But except for an occasional schooner, I wasn't aware of the halibut."

"Yes; it is extensive. I know that the salmon fishery in its heyday was the largest fishery in the United States, commanding a lot of attention. The halibut fishery is a more traditional industry. The halibut fishermen originally came from Norway, to the North Atlantic and now to the Northwest. They fish the North Pacific all the way to the Bering Sea."

"Is that right?" Elmer asked.

"Yes," Harold said. "They opened a fish freezing plant at Taku Harbor in 1902. The first of its kind."

Elmer looked steadily at Harold. "You say they fished out Norway, and then the North Atlantic, and now they're hitting the North Pacific?"

Harold sobered. "I didn't say that exactly, but yes, for all practical purposes, that's true. However, there have been many efforts made not to repeat that in the North Pacific by both the United States and Canada." Harold looked ready to explain in detail, but the mood of the evening had become too serious for Elmer. He'd looked forward to the pleasure of this journey for some time. Harold Lokken certainly knew his business, and at another time, Elmer would like to be educated about the halibut fishery. But not this evening.

"I'm sure it's interesting," Elmer said. "Another time, perhaps."

Harold's expression grew withdrawn and blank. "Yes, indeed; far too serious for such an occasion," he said. He raised his wine glass to the table and smiled.

Sitting at a dinner table not too far away, a man in his mid-thirties listened. Having stated that he was a halibut fisherman, others at the table had asked a stream of questions about the industry. He was a fisherman, and a good one, but he was not a historian and was embarrassed that he could not answer. He turned to point toward the captain's table and said to the others at his table, "There's a man who knows all about the halibut fishery. You can ask him all those questions." His name was Oscar Dyson; he was from the East Coast, and had moved to Alaska to satisfy his longtime dream of fishing.

"Being a fisherman is no small chore. We have many concerns—too many to spend time sitting around thinking about the history or the science or any of that. There are a million details to going fishing," he declared in self-defense. "Not to mention the responsibility to the crew," he added.

Queen Charlotte Sound was relatively calm. They crossed during the night, with the ship rising and falling slowly over the long swells rolling in from the Pacific.

The first port for the SS *Aleutian* was Ketchikan.

Ketchikan's shore was strung with docks and piers that served as roads. Houses stacked up the hillside in a visually haphazard way, spilling down to the shore, where a skirt of vessels of every description, from small skiffs to the most beautiful huge schooners, were moored with now and then a larger steamship. It hardly seemed possible that there was room for the SS *Aleutian* to dock.

The captain stood at the station beside the pilothouse, giving orders to the men below in a quiet but firmly polite voice. "Ready with the spring line, Mr. Rollins. Ready to the port bow, Mr. Jones." Finally, he ordered, "Mr. Smith, ready to the stern," as the ship slid into place beside the pier.

The lines were thrown and fastened, the gangway was lowered, and passengers poured off the ship to investigate the town or to disembark with packages and bundles. Scores of people stood on the pier to greet the arrival whether they were meeting someone or not. It was an occasion.

A small delegation stood on the pier, scanning the line of faces above the rail of the ship for Elmer Rasmuson, waving wildly when they saw him appear among the rest. He waved and made his way to the exit.

Clem and Jim were among the first down the ramp. "You headed for Creek Street?" one of the passengers yelled after the two young men. Several people laughed.

"What's that?" Clem asked.

"Beats me, but it must be awfully funny," Jim replied.

They learned it was the district where the prostitutes were. They went and looked from the bridge at the tiny shacks on stilts along the small stream, and laughed self-consciously at even being there to look. They headed back to the docks to look at the fishing boats.

Standing above a lower pier, looking down at the boats below, they listened to two old men sitting on the hatch of a halibut schooner. They were sharpening hooks. The sound of their voices mingled with the cry of the gulls overhead, and the engine sounds of boats, winches, and outboard motors.

One man leaned forward and spoke to the other in a loud voice. "By God, it's ruined. All them short-termers, school teachers, and such. They think they're fishermen just because they got a boat. They don't know a damn thing about it."

"Ah, come on, Ole; the season's shorter, but we got a lot of fish."

"Yeah? Well, you watch. This will go the same as the sardines went. Everyone's already forgot there was a sardine fishery. We went from millions of pounds to nothing in ten years, and every year they talked about how the fish would come back. Blaming the decline on every reason they could dream up except over fishing. It's enough to make you puke."

"I guess if you were one of them you wouldn't have too much to say about it."

"You're right about that. But one fisherman doesn't change it. I'm a fisherman. If the law says you can fish, I'll fish. That doesn't mean I'm blind."

"What about the International Halibut Commission? Their quar-

26

ters are right at the University of Washington with all those fisheries scientists. What about the Fishing Vessel Owners Association in Seattle? They're always trying to figure some way to manage it."

Ole hunkered down over the tub of hooks, silent for a time. "I hope your attitude proves more right than mine," he growled.

"You have to believe that all that effort comes to some good. After all, if we don't have any more fish, they're out of business, right?"

Jim Branson turned to leave, bumping into Oscar Dyson, who was standing a few feet away and taking in the scene on the schooner. Jim backed up and mumbled an apology, but Oscar ignored that and, pointing to the vessel below, stated flatly, cheeks turning pink and eyes blazing with anger, "Listen to that sourpuss! The average catch was almost sixty thousand pounds. If there's anything I can't stand, it's a whiner. Name's Oscar Dyson. I fish halibut, too." And he stomped away.

Onboard the SS *Aleutian* again, Oscar found Harold and Alice Lokken.

"Excuse me, sir," Oscar addressed Harold politely. "I couldn't help but overhear your conversation at dinner last night. Down on the wharf today I overheard a fisherman complaining that the halibut stocks are being ruined. Going the way of the sardine. Can that be true?"

Harold studied the man in front of him. Spotted him as an easterner by his slight accent. "We are trying our very best to ensure that history does not repeat itself. As you know, the East hasn't done a very good job. We hope to learn from that. I could tell you what is being done." He added, "I assume you're a halibut fisherman."

"I am. I know there are several agencies working on the problem, and I could tell that you're an expert. Thanks a lot for the reassurance," Oscar said. "I'd love to hear about it, but I have to meet a guy." He walked down the deck and into the corridor to go to his stateroom below.

Harold turned to Alice and remarked, "That's the usual problem. They don't have time to think about it."

As the ship made its way up the Inland Passage fish traps were sprinkled along with their fleets of big flat-bottomed skiffs tied nearby on the beach. Occasionally they would see a large boat tied alongside, the web being lifted and emptied with brails into the hold of the boat that was the tender, to then be taken to the cannery for canning.

Harold and Alice stood at the rail beside other passengers, fascinated by the passing scene. They moved closer, but kept a discreet distance from one of the ship's crew, who was explaining the way the salmon traps worked.

"You can see how that long row of piling runs out into deep water. These are called the lead. There is a net that hangs from them, making a fence, if you will, that leads the fish into the trap. That big square of pilings not only has a web around its perimeter, but a huge web that lies on the whole bottom of it. When the fish have been led into the trap and are confused by the baffled entrance, they circle and circle there until the boat, called a tender, comes and lifts the web from the bottom, now called a brail, and pours the fish into the hold of the tender. The net is then returned to the bottom of the trap to wait for the next batch of fish."

"They can't fish every day all summer, can they? That would scoop up all the fish," one of the passengers asked.

"No, no. There are designated days. I think maybe it is Monday through Friday," their informant replied. "Then the web is all lifted up above the water so the fish can swim right past the pilings."

"The local folks that own these fish traps must make a lot of

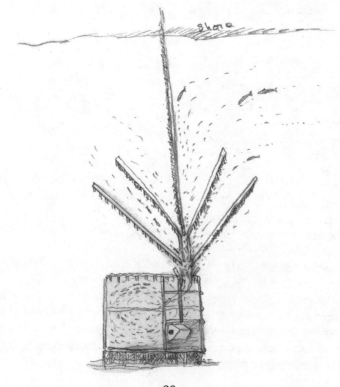

28

money," Alice observed, as the ship moved slowly by one being emptied. "That's a lot of fish."

"Ninety-nine percent are owned by companies in Seattle or San Francisco. Alaska doesn't have the wealth to finance the setup necessary to fund such an operation. I suppose someday they will," Harold replied.

"Come along, Alice; let's go to the lounge," Harold said, taking Alice by the arm and moving away from the rail.

Clem Tillion had slowly made his way into the first-class lounge, ignoring the rule about steerage passengers, and struck up a conversation with Tom Wardleigh. He learned a little bit about flying from the young pilot. They were the same age, but Tom, in his quiet way, seemed older. He was established in his field, and doing it. Clem impressed him with his knowledge of the war and of his tenure in the South Pacific. Tom listened.

Bob Thorstenson and Lee Alverson gravitated to the conversation. Lee occasionally took the stage, balancing his wartime stories of China against Clem's South Pacific ones and talking resource management, and Clem listened. Harold Lokken stayed on the perimeter of these discussions. Lee deferred to him occasionally, but he always gave the briefest of statements. Oscar hung around the perimeter of these conversations but contributed little. Jim Branson joined them when they gathered on deck. He was not comfortable about breaking the steerage passenger rules to that extent.

One evening while strolling around the lower deck, Tom held out his arm to stop. "Shh. Hear that?"

They were silent. From the stern they could hear what seemed to be muffled, angry words and scuffling.

Tom moved over against the side of the ship, sliding along the wall toward the sound; Clem and Jim followed. At the corner, they heard a mumbling voice screaming, "No, no! That's not who I am! I'm a fisherman! I tell you, I'm a fisherman!"

More scuffling. "You rotten bastard! We know who you are. It's you and your kind who never wet their feet but tell us what we can do. By God we don't need people like you," was the harshly whispered reply.

They peered around the corner just in time to see two men grapple another almost to the deck. "I think they are beating up on Mr. Lokken. He's a big wheel with the halibut fishermen," Tom Wardleigh whispered.

One had an arm lock on the victim's neck, and the other was trying to loop a line around his hands behind his back. The victim bit down on the arm around his throat and at the same time jammed backward,

pressing the other man against the wall, forcing him to let go of the line to try to extricate himself from the pressure. The bitten man screamed and let go. The victim, who they now saw was Oscar Dyson, spun around, grabbing both men by the scruff of the neck, and banged their heads together, again and again, then threw them across the deck, where they crashed against the rail. One grabbed the rail to hold himself upright, and the other fell to the deck.

Clem, Tom, and Jim dashed around the corner toward Oscar. Seeing the three men come into view, the two assailants staggered away. Jim followed, to determine which cabin they would go to, so there would be some way to identify them. He followed them into the hall and down the narrow stair to a lower cabin. When they had gone inside he sidled up to the door. Through the vent he could hear one swearing. "Damn you, you said Lokken was a puny bookkeeper! The SOB damn near bit my arm off, and I swear my nose is busted. I should knock your block off."

The other man whimpered, "Honest, Oblensky told me he was a wimp. He said he couldn't see how such a wimpy guy could have so much power and influence."

Jim Branson noted the number of the room, tiptoed back to the stairs, raced up and onto the deck, and back to the stern. Oscar was saying, "Well, sure. I can see how guys might get mad about the regulations but that seems a little extreme. Mr. Lokken must be a very important man to think throwing him overboard would change the way things are going."

Jim came running back on deck. Out of breath, he gasped, "I got their cabin number. We'd better find Mr. Lokken. They still think it was him. Boy, were they surprised. We'd better tell him to be careful."

"Be sure Mrs. Lokken isn't nearby. No sense scaring her," Tom warned.

"Let's go up to the lounge. They might be there," Clem said, starting to move in that direction. "You coming, Oscar?"

"No; I think I'll go back to my cabin."

"I'll come along with you," Tom volunteered.

In the lounge they found Harold, Alice, and Elmer sitting at a table having a nightcap. Their conversation was animated, if the gestures were any indication.

"What a shame to tell him," Clem whispered.

"We have to," Jim said.

They stood watching the scene in the room—a tranquil scene, with the sound of cheerful voices, backed by the muted melody from the jukebox.

Harold, as though feeling their concentration, turned and looked their way. Clem made a gesture of "come" to him. Harold stood up and walked toward them, weaving in and out around the tables, nodding to one person and then another.

When he reached the place where Clem and Jim stood, Jim stepped between him and their table, blocking Alice's view of their faces. "We have to tell you that Oscar Dyson was attacked back in the stern of the ship on the lower deck by two guys who thought he was you. They were really mad."

Harold stared at them, his face frozen with a fierce, angry expression.

"It's okay; probably halibut fishermen who have protested the proposed layup program. They'll be drunk and mean. It won't really lead to anything. We're proposing that each vessel lay up for seven days after delivery before going out again. I'm sorry about the other fellow getting banged up for it. Thanks for telling me. I will be careful." He held out his hand.

"It looked like they were going to throw you overboard. I think this is pretty serious and we should report them. I have the number of their cabin," Jim Branson said.

Harold looked at the eager young man. "Your interest is to be commended, but, no, the best thing is to let it go. They will be half sober by now and by morning will be trying to forget it." Harold turned away from them and returned to the table. He didn't look back.

"I think that's one tough man," Jim stated.

"I suspect he's been in that situation before," Clem said.

Tom was coming up the deck when they went out. "Did you find him? What did he say?" he asked.

"Just thanked us. Said he figured they were mad, drunk fishermen who blamed him for some regulation."

They stood along the rail looking at the starry night, each turning over the events of the evening in his own mind.

Having heard whispered comments about the event of the night before, Elmer approached the three young men where they were lounging on deck. "What was all that about last night? This afternoon I overheard a conversation that sounded like someone had attacked Mr. Lokken. I haven't seen him today. Have you?"

Clem laughed, "True enough. Two fellows did attack who they thought was Mr. Lokken, but they had the wrong man."

"Right," Jim added. "They thought they had a bookkeeper and found out they'd attacked a wolverine. Oscar Dyson tossed them around like basketballs. I tracked them down to find their room but Mr. Lokken wouldn't let us do anything about it. He just figured they were drunk and mad."

Elmer chuckled, "I think Harold Lokken's reputation is going to increase a bit from now on, however." Sobering instantly, he said, "That is a serious thing. I do think, if you know who they are, that something should be done."

"The most important thing here is that those fellows don't find out that they hit the wrong man. I'd say that Mr. Lokken is quite safe with his new reputation," Tom Wardleigh said with a big smile. "In fact, I'd volunteer that his fame is spreading as we speak." He laughed again, envisioning the late-night story hour at the local pub, wherever it may be.

The ship pulled into Wrangell, and Jim Branson hurried down the gangway after a very brief farewell. He was excited.

"Hope you find what you're looking for," Jim said to Clem.

"So do I," Clem replied.

Petersburg was the next port of call. Clem thought he saw the two men disembark, two bundled-up creatures hurrying down the ramp to duck behind a stack of freight.

Clem ran down the ramp after them and rushed to the mound of boxes. He slowly slipped along the side to the corner, hoping to hear or see something of their intentions.

"Now what are we going to do?" one angry voice was growling, barely above a whisper. "Do we have to stand here behind these boxes, for God's sake?"

"No, no," the other man replied. "Oblensky said he'd have a cab here for us."

"Well, he'd better, or he'll be the one over the side. This is the stupidest thing I've ever gotten into!" the first voice snarled.

"Hush!" the other man said.

Clem stayed pressed tightly against the huge stack of freight until he heard an auto drive nearby and stop. He heard its horn honking and peered around the corner in time to see the two men climb into the taxi.

The SS *Aleutian* reached Juneau two days later. It was a real parting of the ways for Clem, as Lee, Bob, Harold and Alice, and Tom Wardleigh disembarked.

Clem stood at the rail, watching them carry their things down the gangway and waving good-bye from the wharf below.

"Weird to feel like you know someone so well after such a brief time," Clem said out loud to himself.

He walked around the streets of Juneau. The town was so small. It seemed impossible that it could be the capitol city of the territory of Alaska. The Territorial Legislative Session had just ended and the capitol building, with its massive pillars of marble, was vacant of the activity it held not long before. The office of the governor and the Alaska Territorial Museum remained active in the building.

Rasmuson came striding out of the building, bounding down the steps at a fast pace, intent on his mission. Seeing Clem and recognizing him, Elmer smiled and nodded, but continued down the street.

The trip across the Gulf of Alaska was a study in how seasick a person can get. When they pulled into Prince William Sound after stops at Cordova and Valdez, Clem was eager for the sight of Resurrection Bay and Seward, where he, too, would disembark.

Prior to making the trip to Alaska, Clem had read copious volumes and bulletins sent to him from his friend Paul Becker in New Jersey, about Alaska. Paul had delved them out of the Smithsonian and the Armed Services Institute. It seemed that the Kenai Peninsula was the most interesting, with good agricultural opportunities, good harbors, and inland seas. Clem took the train to Anchorage. After pacing the dusty streets and tempted by the descriptions of the Kenai, he hopped the train to Seward, to jump off near Moose Pass and to follow what was indicated as a trail on the map he carried. He walked to the Kenai Peninsula and then walked the 170 miles to Seldovia.

The "trail," which at best, was vague, always ended at the water's edge. The trail was apparently one made for winter dog team traffic when the waters were frozen.

It took six weeks to traverse over 170 miles of hills and around the shore of Kachemak Bay, hitching a ride on a boat to the town of Seldovia, on the south shore.

In Seldovia, Clem met a man going to Halibut Cove Lagoon in a big skiff. He went along for the fun of it.

Clem Tillion knew that he had found what he wanted when he saw Halibut Cove. He knew he had to work to get a boat of his own.

A year later, in his own big skiff, he pulled into the Cove and stopped alongside a fishing vessel where three men sat talking.

The men ignored his presence completely. He sat on the gunnel of his skiff and waited.

A tall, slender man in a cowboy hat finally turned and questioned, "Wha'da'ya' want, kid?"

"I just wanted to say hello," Clem said, his voice breaking a little in his eagerness.

"Well, come on aboard," the cowboy drawled. They stared at him as he climbed aboard the fishing boat. The three men turned back to their conversation, ignoring him again, but he was happy sitting on the large gunnel, feet on deck, listening.

A woman came out of the cabin. Clem could smell food.

"What did you say your name was?" the woman asked.

"Clem Tillion," he replied with a big grin.

The conversation of the men hesitated, just long enough to hear the name, then continued.

"Well, Red," she said, "my name's Ada Latham. Come on in for a bite of lunch." She beckoned for the others to follow. Clem hadn't really looked over the men on the deck, not wanting them to think he was being too intrusive. But when he went down into the galley, he was stunned to see that one of them was familiar. "Say, aren't you Oscar Dyson? Didn't I see you on the *Aleutian* not too long ago?"

"Well, I'll be darned. You sure did. That's who I am. I live here."

Clem sighed. That was thirty-three years ago. It seemed impossible that so much time had passed. Oscar did look a little older, with a few gray hairs, but really he didn't look much different. He looked around the room.

Council members were still shuffling through the scientific committee's reports. At the nod of the chairman's head, one of the members asked a question of one of the scientific committee, triggering a lengthy reply.

Clem slipped back into his recall, remembering going halibut fishing with Oscar Dyson on his boat, *Roxana Dawn*.

Everyone called him "Red" when he was ashore and "Tillionson" while he was on the halibut boat. The rest of the crew were Dyson, Nelson, and Robinson. Only Nelson was Scandinavian but they were all pleased to have their names end in "son," like the boys in the classic fleet.

The fishing had gone well in spite of the weather.

The North Pacific Ocean houses a tremendous halibut fishery. In 1948, that fishery lasted from April until August. The season was determined by allowable poundage designated by the Halibut Commission and called the MSY (maximum sustainable yield). During the months of the halibut season, a chain of vessels from the crudest to the most beautiful and graceful of schooners were sprinkled along the length of the North Pacific Ocean. Onboard these halibut boats, the crew stood in stylized position to play their role in the pattern of activity.

Each one of these jobs was critical to the whole operation. If one man was sloppy or inattentive to his role, the domino effect took place, and the rest of the crew were heartless in rebuttal.

To be a good crew member on a halibut boat was a matter of great pride. They worked hard and long hours, taking as little time to eat and sleep as could be squeezed out of the day.

One afternoon, near the end of the season, Oscar stood at the roller on the vessel's rail, watching the line come in, poised for the next hook, hypnotized by the motion, and eager for what might be on it. He leaned far over. "There's a big one coming!" he yelled. "Slack off!" The crewman coiling the gear loosened the tension on the ground line, letting it slip in position on the gurdy, stopping the incoming motion.

"Hey, Red, bring the rifle! Bring another gaff hook."

Red rushed to the cabin and reached for the .22 rifle, grabbing for another gaff. He then swung back out to the edge of the boat, where Oscar stood, peering over the side. Red checked the chamber to be sure a bullet was in it. He peered over the side, too.

Oscar motioned for a slow tug on the ground line, without taking his eye off the incoming line. The coiler slowly pulled, keeping the speed at half, watching Oscar for other signs of instruction. The *Roxana Dawn* surged up and down in the long swell. Oscar rarely got excited even when the tension was extreme.

Red leaned far over the gunnel trying to see the fish. "Holy cow," Red gasped, as the big fish reached the surface.

The great mass of the fish looked like a huge gray tabletop, limp in the water, seeming to float to the surface. Oscar paused for just a second, staring in awe at the size of the fish, before reaching over to sink in the gaff.

Red raised the rifle to shoot, but the seconds lost in wonderment brought the big fish to life. Arching its back, head, and tail up, it slapped down. With that slap, it flew into the air, spinning around at the same time.

The two men, caught off balance, grabbed for the line, the rifle fell onto the deck, and the gaff Oscar had poised to strike flew through the air and overboard, landing unnoticed, and sank out of sight.

The great fish spun and thrashed. "Gaff, gaff!" Oscar shouted.

Red swung with the gaff, time and again, but he only grazed the frenzied fish.

"Slack off, slack off!" Oscar shouted again.

The coiler slowly but surely let the line back out, carefully guiding the empty hooks around the gurdy. They fell back over the roller as the huge fish sank back into the depths of the sea.

"We'll let her go until she quiets down. When she stops, we'll hold," Oscar said, sitting down on the edge of the hatch.

Five minutes later, they started to pull the fish back toward the boat.

"Put the gaffs here," Oscar said, indicating the edge of the checker bin, where they would be within easy reach of the roller.

Red hung the gaff he held on the lip of the checker bin and went after the other, still hanging from the rack on the back of the cabin.

Red picked up the rifle and brushed it off.

They watched, poised for action, as the huge, dark mass began to appear from the depths below.

Seagulls gathered overhead, drawn by the excitement. They circled, watching.

"Look at that big devil," Oscar gloated. "She'll top off this trip."

"She's four hundred pounds if she's an ounce," Red stated.

The fish slowly came to the side of the boat. It had been hanging out flat, but now it slowly sank, hanging downward, alongside, seemingly limp and lifeless.

"Now!" Oscar yelled.

Red lifted the rifle, Oscar swung the gaff, and Nelson stood by with another gaff, ready to assist. Red's gaff hung over the edge of the checker bin to be grabbed, as soon as he shot the fish, and a spare gaff hung beside it. The coiler began to slowly reel the line in, watching the three men at the gunnel.

The fish exploded, sending Oscar's gaff flying through the air, spinning in circles, landing with a splash far from the boat. The blast of the rifle was as ineffectual as the bullet that hit the massive body of the fish, instead of the vital head section. Red grabbed for the gaff and swung. The fish spun and flopped, knocking the gaff into the air, and Red's swinging arm crashed against the side of the boat, where he hung over the side like a rag.

Nelson reached far over the side to swing his gaff. It fell home, right into the big head of the fish. They all yelled an incoherent scream of victory as he pulled upward. But the power of the huge body in the water exerted itself, seeming to rise as if to come aboard. Then it spun and lurched backward, twisting the gaff out of Nelson's hand and tossing it like a scrap of debris to one side. Giving one last violent twist, the fish broke the gangion, and sank below the surface of the sea.

The crew of the *Roxana Dawn* stood dripping wet and stunned, staring at the blank surface of the water, engulfed by the sudden silence, save for the rhythmic hum of the diesel engine and the cry of the gulls.

Oscar looked desperately around. Frustration and anger seeking an outlet. He spotted the last gaff hanging on the checker bin. He leaned over, grabbed it, and threw it with all his strength. "Here, you . . . you . . . louse bound, lily livered son of a sea cook, you forgot one!" he screamed.

The gaff turned slowly as it flew through the air, landing with a splash.

The crew set about their chores, not wanting to look at each other

39

for fear they would either laugh or cry, and prayed the last of the catch were small enough to get aboard without a gaff.

Oscar turned to the crew, daring them to complain about the loss of the last gaff. "Well, we're pretty well loaded, anyway," he said. He indicated to the coiler to bring the line in again, and they all prayed the last of the fish would be small enough to get aboard.

As surely as the fish were hooked by them, Red was hooked on fish.

Two

Executive Director Branson was remembering his first fisheries experience in Alaska.

As he'd stepped aboard the small patrol boat at Wrangell, in Southeast Alaska, Jim Branson had been more than a little overwhelmed by the job he'd so quickly accepted as a U.S. Fish and Wildlife Service enforcement officer, in waters he'd never seen before, and among people he didn't know.

He'd felt confident in Oregon where he had been fishing on his own boat along that open coast. The job sounded easy compared to the intermittent terror that his very old two-cylinder Atlas engine had provided. "Scared ourselves out of our wits," his partner confided many years later. But now, with the full force of this new adventure before him, it didn't seem simple at all, regardless of the first-rate equipment.

As he stepped aboard with his new superior, firm resolve was registered in his expression. "Here are the charts of your area. You'll want to acquaint yourself with basic channels. The creek robbers exercise a bit more daring than you'll care to tackle," the man explained.

Jim nodded and bent down to examine the engine. *What did the guy think he was, a pansy?* The boat was small, but it was perfect. He took a deep breath and stood up. "Yes, sir," he said as he took the charts. He couldn't wait to get these preliminaries over with. In spite of the awesome responsibility, it beat the heck out of working on a chicken farm which he had done to get out of debt. Of course, a year in college had been fun. His handsome, yet shy, charm made him a definite ladies choice. But this . . . this was adventure . . . adventure with authority.

"Take her out and get the feel of it; locate those spawning streams

41

marked here in red. They will be the targets of the creek robbers," the boss continued.

"Yes, sir," Jim acknowledged (as if he didn't know).

Later, writing to his girlfriend, he said, "There is no way to describe the beauty of this place. Yesterday I almost made my first arrest. I guess he heard my engine. Oh, well."

One evening while walking along the street in Wrangell, a voice called after him as he passed the doorway of a local bar. "You want a creek robber, fish hawk?"

He stopped and turned, resentful of the tone of voice when the man said "fish hawk" (the name given to enforcement officers), but kept his cool. "Sure thing," he replied.

"Well, you'll find one at Copper Creek . . . high tide. They'll be there," the man stated, and started to chuckle as he turned away. "They'll be there, all right." Then he disappeared behind the door.

The creek robbers were fishermen who fished above the markers set at the mouth of a stream or river, a stop sign to the fishermen to not fish upstream where the fish were spawning. The creek robbers watched for the creek mouths that could accommodate a seine boat at the top of the flood tide, and also accommodate the huge schools of fish waiting off the mouth of the stream to rush into their spawning grounds.

Jim studied the chart, studied the tide book. It would be dusk at high tide.

He listened to the sound of his engine at every speed, seeking the quietest. That drunk would laugh his head off if he missed; and yet, perhaps it was a scam and he was laughing now. He was damned if he did and damned if he didn't give it a try.

The chart showed that the mouth of the creek was nestled beside a rocky point with a sheer, high bluff. Motoring to it seemed to take hours—hours ridden with the fear that he was being tagged and was walking into a trap of some sort. He found a location to wait out of sight of the stream mouth.

Jim's heart was already pounding from excitement, even though he had a long time to wait—a long time to wonder if they would kill him or beat him up. Or just what would they do? There were lots of stories of the enforcement officer who never came back. The five-hour wait was the longest time of his life.

As dusk arrived, the creek edge along the bluff was in total shadow. There was no moon. He'd run the stream earlier, so he knew it was safe to pull around the point and follow the edge of the bank. At the

peak of the tide, he started the engine and slowly moved into the dark shadows.

Jim was amazed at how complete the darkness was. He peered out of the window, trying to see an edge, or something—anything. Suddenly there was a loud thump, thump, thump along the edge of the hull as the bow of the boat struck some floating debris. The sound was unbelievably loud. They would hear him. In a panic, he put the shift in neutral, taking the engine out of gear.

He leaned out of the window to try to discern what it was. He heard low voices and quickly grabbed the switch on the spotlight.

He was inside the set of a creek robber. The debris he had encountered was the cork line of the set. It encircled his patrol boat, just as it would the salmon under the water.

He was caught.

He heard one of them yell, "Fish hawk; let 'em go; let's get out of here."

"Jesus, man," another replied. "It's too late; maybe we can bribe the guy, or talk our way out of this."

"Let's shoot the bastard," another one yelled, dashing for the cabin.

"No; no, you don't. Creek robbing's one thing. Murder's another," another man stated firmly.

"That must be the skipper," Jim thought.

Jim pulled alongside. His heart was pounding so hard he could hardly breathe. His hand was shaking and he could barely manage the controls. He'd heard the man yell, "Shoot!" and figured he'd had it. This was it, but this was better than having that drunk laugh at him.

He pulled alongside. "Dump the fish, and come with me," he said in the loudest, meanest voice he could muster.

Then he saw that there was another fishing boat just beyond the first. He shone the spotlight on them and shouted the same order again.

"Pull it in," the skipper ordered. They let the lead lines go overboard and began to haul in the net without a word.

Jim went aboard. He recorded the names of the crew on each vessel. They were sullen and made no move to resist. He would learn that one of the crew of the second boat hid in the fo'c'sle. He was apprehended later.

Jim was totally amazed. He'd ordered and they had obeyed. They would follow him into Wrangell.

When he brought them in, the guy at the bar gave himself full credit, but Jim Branson was no longer considered a rookie. Jim heard that even in Juneau the crew at the U.S. Fish and Wildlife Service office roared with glee when they heard the news.

At the council table, Jim smiled to himself. Clem glanced his way. Seeing his expression, he leaned over and asked, "What's so funny?"

"Nothing here. I was just remembering my first 'fish hawk' adventure. I'll tell you about it later." He turned his attention back to the man who was speaking. The man was explaining material to the audience that Jim, as executive director, had already studied.

The meeting droned on.

Clem asked for the status of the Individual Fishing Quotas proposal. He knew what it was but wanted the report to be expressed at the meeting. It was under review.

In the audience, Bob Thorstenson, who represented Icicle Seafoods and was a member of the International North Pacific Fisheries Commission, looked down at the sheets and volumes of data on his lap. The same papers were on the table in front of each of the council members. He had gathered them off the table near the door as he came in.

The chairman's mention of the trauma attached to the fishing industry caused his expression to change from one of professional blankness to amused irony in recall. He was not seeing the papers in his lap now; he was seeing the yard sale, in Petersburg, 1965, when they were desperately trying to get their act together to start Petersburg Fisher-

ies. He was hearing his lovely young wife urging people to buy things she had just acquired.

Some folks had laughed. "He isn't dancing up a storm now; he's sweating over getting the money together." There may have been a tinge of envy to the remark. Bob was in great demand at parties and on the dance floor. Pam, his young wife, was as beautiful as any movie star so the two of them seemed unreal. Pam's mother had warned her, "Be careful" (when Pam had remarked, "That's the man I'm going to marry."). She continued her warning, "Every girl wants to marry him. He's too handsome for his own good. He's a playboy. You be careful."

The cannery was for sale because the salmon had been so over-fished and mismanaged canneries were no longer the gold mine they had been. In 1965, the cannery that was vital to the town of Petersburg was up for sale. If it did not sell, it would be a disaster to the economy of the town.

Just the year before, Governor Egan had invited the Japanese to come into the state and buy salmon because the fishermen would not settle on the price with their American companies who were backing out of the salmon industry. A few canneries did join partnerships with the Japanese. The king crab fishery was booming and the halibut fishery was stabilized by the International Halibut Commission.

The salmon industry was no longer the mega-million-dollar business it had been. Salmon canneries were being sold or abandoned all along the coast of Alaska.

Being a cannery accountant had taught Bob Thorstenson the details of the industry. He'd overheard the company men decide to sell the cannery—"just to get out from under," they'd said. With statehood in 1958, the traps that had scooped up the salmon runs with little complication had been banned. The cannery owners grumbled. "We can't deal with all these piddling fishermen and their whims and problems. It's time to get out. These folks are going to learn that having statehood and getting rid of the salmon traps is not going to be the answer to their problems; it'll be the beginning. They can't catch enough fish to make a cannery a growing concern with their hokey outfits. It's over."

Later, Bob made a phone call. "Come over to the office this evening, about seven," Bob urged Magnus Martens, his father-in-law. "They'll think I'm working late. I have something to propose."

"If it's about Pam, you'd better come to the house," Martens said.

Bob held up both hands in a negative gesture. "No, no; this is fish business."

"Okay, but why not meet in the café? The office isn't exactly comfortable," Magnus Martens objected.

"Because others can hear us," Bob replied, with urgency in his voice.

Bob went back to the office to prepare a financial sheet that should cover any question that Magnus might ask. He knew Magnus would be thorough. If Magnus could see a way, then he, Bob, would have to find some way to come up with his share of the money. Sell his herd of cattle at Point Roberts, for one thing. It made his stomach hurt just to think of it. His beautiful cows at his family's farm. It seemed disloyal to his heritage there. That herd represented his continued presence on the land he grew up knowing.

He was right. Magnus was thorough. Bob explained about the proposed sale and showed the spreadsheet of financial status and potential debt.

Magnus didn't say anything at first.

He looked out the window. "You know, it's a funny thing about money. I did real well most of the time. There were always expenses; much of it went for gear or a new boat. I was really surprised when I found out my wife had bought a piece of land to build a house on when I was out on a halibut trip. She must have had a few dollars stowed away that I didn't know about," Magnus said. He smiled at Bob. "You just never know. You think you're in charge and they go and do something like that. We had to build a house, of course. One thing leads to another," he added in a thoughtful voice. Bob waited. What was the problem? How did he get off on the story about the house? "There must have been something I didn't make clear and he's being polite," Bob thought. He picked up the papers to explain again.

"No, no; put the papers down. I guess this is kind of like the house, and I was just figuring who else could come up with some of it. Not build the whole house ourselves. Say, a quarter of a half of it," he said in a matter-of-fact voice. "I'll talk to Gordon and Thompson. You can get the rest from the bank."

"From the bank?" Bob gasped. "To buy a cannery now? I don't know."

"Well, you asked me to invest. If you think it's good enough for my money . . . or yours . . . yours and Pam's, you must think it's good enough for the bank," Magnus said matter-of-factly. "I'll talk to the fellows." He stood up to leave. The conversation was over.

Bob stood up, extending his hand. Magnus had put him on the spot. No bank money, no deal. That would be the proof of his idea. Not to mention how he'd raise his share.

Bob saw them coming toward the door of the office early the next morning. Singly, they were impressive enough, but in a group, they were overwhelming. Gordon towered over the other two, but it wasn't

just a matter of size. They walked like men who would get where they were going. Bob would have to hold up his end for sure. He had been so certain. But would they see flaws that he didn't see?

They studied the financial layout that Bob had prepared. They talked about trip limits on halibut, prices of cod, and salmon market potential. It was getting better . . . slowly. The absence of the traps had been a boon to the salmon seiners. But people were getting out of the cannery business, not getting into it. They talked about the "old days." "I started out with a bang," Martens said. "The first year, my crew walked off with a seventy-dollar crew share." He looked around. "You have to realize that a sack of flour cost twenty-five cents then."

Gordon Jensen smiled. "I remember when the fishery was so small, I went to Seattle to the Union and Vessel Owners meetings. We met in Harold Lokken's office, and when he asked, 'Who represents the vessel owners?' I said, 'I do.' When he asked, 'Who represents the Union?' I said, 'I do.' It was real personal then."

It looked like this could go on all morning. Bob, trying to not sound desperate, pushed the papers forward a little. "Well?" he asked. Then he added, "The workday will begin here before long," indicating the cannery and its attendant business.

"Looks like a good idea," Gordon said. "There is one thing, though, that I think we should consider here about the bookkeeper."

Bob's heart sank; he would be voted out of it!

"Yes?"

"I think we should do it like on a boat. The captain gets a boat share because he runs the show and takes all the responsibility for that. I think that's how we should set this thing up. Bob, here, will have all that headache. I think he should get a boat share, a percent of the profit over expenses, besides the regular dividend of a shareholder."

The other two men looked thoughtful.

Bob was stunned. "My word. I can't do that . . . you don't realize what that could mean."

Gordon smiled. "I think we do," he said. "We might call it an incentive factor. Is it agreed?" he asked.

They agreed.

Hat in hand, Bob went from bank to bank.

Begging was a new experience. But failure was unacceptable. Having exhausted all financial institutions, he went to Juneau to see if there was any sort of state loan program available.

Uninterested bureaucrats, in seemingly endless numbers, passed him along to yet another department. In desperation, he finally went to the governor's office.

"Petersburg," he pleaded, "depends on the cannery. No one wants to buy a cannery now. The day of the salmon is over, and yet I am confident we can make a go of this if we can just get a loan. I am not asking for charity . . . just a loan."

The governor listened. He believed this ardent young man.

Petersburg, he knew, was a stable community of fishermen.

"Wait here," the governor said, standing up to first phone and then to leave, having assured himself the person he wanted to see was there.

Bob sat slumped over in the chair. He'd wanted to talk longer, to be more persuasive. He was sure the governor would just go get the "no" from someone else so he wouldn't be the bad guy to do it.

When the door of the office opened, Bob leaped to his feet.

"This gentleman will help you," the governor said, indicating his companion. "There are some disaster funds available. I think for Petersburg to lose the cannery would be a disaster, indeed." He smiled as he shook Bob's hand. Bob sputtered words of thanks. He had no speech of gratitude prepared, even in his mind. He was so used to defeat, but his expression revealed the surprise, delight, and pleasure that the news prompted. The governor then indicated that he was busy, turning away to things on his desk, as Bob followed the other man out the door.

It was over so quickly.

Bob rushed to the phone to relay the news.

Bob looked around the room at the mob of people. Most of them were just as eager and, in some cases, panicky as he had been then. *Times change, but there always seems to be a substantial amount of crises,* he thought. *Maybe not in the halibut fishery. It always seems to be under good control.*

Bob looked at Harold. "How the heck does he do it? He's always calm. If he does get excited, you can't tell from his looks. The inscrutable gentleman."

Harold Lokken, at the council table representing the Vessel Owners Association of Seattle, studied the papers in front of him. Petersburg had a good fleet. Men who took it upon themselves to study the industry, to do well but not without restriction. Like Gordon Jensen over there. But there had been plenty of pain in keeping it under some sort of stable management. Not to mention the stupidity of those fish-

ermen who didn't want any management at all, like that fellow Oblensky, years ago. He's probably dead or in jail. The only advice he ever took was to leave Seattle. He'd never forget how they met.

It was 1936.

Harold had watched the fishermen file into the room. At thirty-one years of age, he was younger than most of the men entering. He was a deliberately quiet young man, and seemed older than his years.

The shuffle and rustle of the men, the scraping of chair legs on the wood floor, as they sat down, suddenly stopped. Their attention now focused on Harold Lokken, their manager and spokesman, seated at the desk at the head of the room (the pulpit, as an irreverent member called it).

Harold looked, with firm expression, at his audience before he began to explain the first item on the agenda. He cleared his throat, sitting very straight, shuffling a sheaf of paper, as if it represented the group and the issues at hand.

"We are here today to talk about the problems associated with the fleet coming into port all at once," he said, "with fish, which puts a glut on the market, allowing the industry total control of the price because the fish have to be sold. However, some of the lower price is fair, because a portion of the fish have had to wait too long to be a first-rate product. Not to mention the problem that the boat yards, the shipwrights, and handymen who work overtime to get the fleet ready to fish then have no employment after the fleet leaves."

"Get to the point; we know all about that," a rude voice from the back of the room interrupted.

Harold continued as if he hadn't heard. "Our committee has discussed this problem at length, and we feel we have a possible solution. A plan to spread out departures and the delivery of the fish, which will increase the quality in the marketplace."

"Sounds like we're being asked to stand in line like little kids on the playground."

Harold sat back in his chair. The meetings were seldom rude, even in disagreement. This was a new voice, and not Norwegian. He waited until the restless murmuring subsided. "In essence, that is exactly what it is. However, we felt it was hardly like children, but like adults finding a way to do the best job possible all the way around."

"Who are 'we'?" another voice asked politely.

"The International Pacific Halibut Commission Conference Board, with members from both the United States and Canada," Harold replied. "We set out a system we call 'The Grand Experiment.' You will leave port at staggered intervals, and consequently the whole chain of

52

events will be spaced out with time to handle each aspect of the fishery to the best advantage. You will get a higher price for your fish and the consumer gets the best possible product over a longer period of time."

The man who had spoken so rudely stood up. He staggered a little, as if intoxicated. "You mean the first guy out gets a good price! He fishes our hole and leaves us the dregs. You can't call that a good deal. It's all well and fine to sit at a desk and tell us what we can and can't do, where we can fish . . . and when. No thanks," he all but shouted, and sat down abruptly, his face red and puffy from the emotional exertion. He wore a black patch over one eye. His heavy accent did not obscure his English words. His voice was resonant and clear.

Other fishermen mumbled assent.

Harold once again waited for the room to quiet down.

"So, what's the deal?" another asked, respectfully, but caution was thick in his voice, as if he hadn't grasped the explanation.

"I don't exactly like it, but I can't disagree with the problem," a fisherman in the front row stated.

"How long between departures?" a big middle-aged man asked.

"We haven't worked that out," Harold said. "That should be for your consideration."

The room burst into a rush of voices. Speculation on the "The Grand Experiment." If it doubled the price of fish, it might be worth it, if they caught as much, but how could they do that if they only fished half the time?

Harold leaned across the table to the man closest to him and asked, "Who's that one-eyed fellow? I don't remember him."

"Oh, him? He's that wild Russian, Oblensky. Old Ole Olsen had him onboard for years. Said he was a good hand, even if he was radical. Died last fall; left Oblensky the boat. Kind of adopted the kid; felt sorry for him, I guess. Escaped from the Revolution, lost an eye in the effort. Must have been hell," was the reply.

"Well, this isn't a revolution," Harold stated flatly. "He'd better take off his boxing gloves." Harold relaxed into his chair to wait while the men in the room grappled with the new idea. When they settled down a bit he said, "Don't make a decision today. Go home; think about it. I suggest you talk about it around the docks and come back for a decision at our next meeting."

That evening at home, Harold looked up when Alice asked, "You're so quiet, Harold. Is something wrong?"

He smiled faintly and shook his head. "No; not really. It is so difficult to think of a way to control the industry and satisfy everyone. I can hardly hope they'll agree to our idea, but it is in their best interest." He was more personally involved in this than he cared to admit. It was an opportunity to make a change to the best interest of everyone for stability. And yet he worked for the boat owners; he was not their boss. He tried to represent their position at all times.

When the owners gathered to vote at the next meeting, Harold's expression, as he faced the room crowded with anxious faces, was blank, unfeeling, and unrevealing of his intense desire to implement this new idea of orderly production. The possible arguments had been hammering around and around in his brain, and now he studied the faces before him. His heart sank when Oblensky strutted into the room with an obvious group of cohorts.

The tension in the room was extreme.

Harold explained the details of the program. The subject was debated at length by the men in the room, following which one of the owners present asked for the floor.

The man rose slowly to his full height of well over six feet. The awareness of the importance of what he was about to say was clearly evident.

The atmosphere in the room fairly rang with the silence as the group waited.

"We fishermen, we skippers," the mover of the motion said, and looked around the room again, "we have decided," he cleared his throat, "we have decided to try the 'The Grand Experiment' for one year." He paused. "At that time, we will vote on it again," he said, and sat down.

Harold looked down, relief flooding through his very being. He waited for the emotion to subside before looking up. To the fishermen in the room, he looked unconcerned, his expression blank as he nodded his acknowledgment to the spokesman.

A group in the back of the room sputtered and mumbled, "We didn't vote. I thought we were going to vote! You can't just do this so ... so ... fast."

"The meeting has spoken," Harold stated. "This decision has been reached by consideration and due process by both the Canadians and our committee, here. The issue is a fact now for one year. We must address the program and make it work for us."

"This meeting is adjourned," Harold stated, and stood up. He walked around the desk and down the aisle, nodding to the men as he passed. He was eager to get away, to be by himself, to enjoy the victory of this change. They would see how advantageous it would be.

As Harold passed the last row of chairs, he brushed against the figure standing closest to the door. The man's elbow shot out to block his way. "You can't shove us around, mister," he growled. "You'll regret this." Harold recognized Oblensky's voice, but did not look around as he pushed past and out of the door.

Harold shook his head in disbelief the next year when the spokesman announced that they simply could not wait around while others were fishing. The Grand Experiment was not acceptable.

Years later, there would be another "layup program," where a vessel would stay at the dock for seven days between trips. But that would, in time, become impossible to monitor, as the fleet expanded along the long North Pacific coast due to the growing coastal population of Alaska and expansion of the fleet from Washington and Oregon.

Harold shook his head, clearing away the recall of that frustration, as he looked at what a fisheries meeting was like forty-five years later. Vessel owners? Yes; and fishermen, processors, politicians, lawyers, lobbyists, and scientists.

Now there were so many licensed halibut boats that the season was down to thirteen days—not a good thing, but the stocks were in good shape. The Halibut Commission sees to that. However, the foreign fleet and the U.S. joint ventures were taking an ever-increasing amount of halibut as bycatch. That was a worry. Those trawlers destroyed so much. He looked down at the sheet in front of him, with the total bycatch poundage of halibut on it. Picking up a pencil, he figured what the 2,704 metric tons meant in pounds.

Harold shook his head, looking at the reams of paper, at the endless data. It revealed the evidence for management needs, but in itself, it was not a solution.

With guarded expression, he scanned the crowd that filled the chairs set in front of the council table, and the mob that completely filled the space behind, making entry into the room each time an awkward shuffle. The problem was as many faceted as the number of people in the room. His gaze riveted on an old man sitting in the third row. He looked familiar. It was an unpleasant reaction. Good grief; it looked like an old version of that man Oblensky. It was as if thinking about him had conjured him up.

The meeting droned on. Hashing over old issues. The new-old issue of overfishing surfacing again. Harold raised his hand. "Mr. Chairman." He was recognized by the chairman. "Let me read a brief statement from Heward Bell's *The Pacific Halibut,* page 103, and I quote: 'If the destruction of young recruits by trawling is not stemmed or stayed promptly, the extinction of the Pacific halibut fishery will be more traumatic and more rapid than was experienced by the halibut stocks and fishery off New England.' End of quote. We have the bycatch data before us. It is shocking," Harold stated.

"That is being addressed. Unfortunately, it takes time for due process, Mr. Lokken; I think you understand that," the chairman replied.

"I do indeed. I just thought I'd put forward a little reminder that the problem is magnifying every day," Harold said.

"The foreign fleet is the major problem," another member said.

"Speaking of that, perhaps we could get some fish hatchery data from the Japanese efforts with the Russians."

The chairman nodded to Mr. Branson, who made a note.

The meeting droned on, with a few more items prior to the beginning of public testimony.

Harold kept looking at that bycatch of halibut figure. It was a lot of fish—fish thrown overboard. He shook his head. His lips, a thin line of distaste at the realization that this poundage was subtracted from the halibut fleet's quota.

The testimony droned on. The intercept fishery, crab quotas, and on and on. They finally came to the last name on the list of persons asked to testify. "Oblensky," Branson called.

The old man rose slowly from his chair in the third row. He rose slowly, but as he approached the desk set up with a microphone for those who wished to testify, his step became spry and purposeful.

Oblensky did not sit down but stood straight and proud.

He looked at each council member before he began to speak. "I'm here," he said in a strong voice, "to protest your observer program. To protest a law that subjects our young folks to the extreme hazards of the great North Pacific and the dangers of its fisheries. Those young people are barely out of school." He made a sweeping gesture, including them all. "You should each cower in shame at the headlines in today's paper. To be party to such a tragedy." He threw the paper down on the desk and stood silent for a moment, then continued, "I challenge you to address this counting of fish in a humane, sensible manner. What are a few unwanted fish compared to a girl's life? I ask you that," he said, his voice getting louder as he progressed.

Harold couldn't bring himself to speak, to acknowledge the distasteful man. He scribbled on his notepaper where he'd figured the poundage and passed it on to the chairman.

Clem looked down at the note, scanning it quickly.

"Mr. Oblensky," he said, "I don't believe that 2,704 metric tons of halibut, not to mention the poundage of other species, is a trivial matter. I suggest that we couldn't agree more with your expressed distress over the accident to the observer. However, no one is forced to do the job, and it is a job that must be done." He added firmly, "If that is the sum total of your testimony, with you being our last person to speak, I would entertain a motion that this meeting adjourn."

Mr. Oblensky's face became rigid. His chin jutted forward as he leaned over to pound the desk with his fist. "I will not be put off," he

shouted. "I demand, as a concerned citizen, that you change the observer regulation to protect the lives of our young men and women."

Clem stood up. "You are repeating yourself, Mr. Oblensky. Your testimony is on record. Good day." He turned to Jim and said, "I believe that is the last person on the list, Mr. Branson," as he gathered his notebooks and papers to leave.

Other members followed suit, turning their attention away from the gallery of attendants, who also were standing and gathering in small groups in the hallway to talk about their subjects of interest.

Oblensky tried to intrude himself into these conversations, but without success. There had been other radical citizens who testified with as much posturing, and they weren't impressed.

Harold had turned his chair completely around, but even with his back toward the front of the room, he could tell just where Oblensky was. The sound of his voice penetrating the soft words of the others made it all too clear, but he wasn't coming closer, thank God.

"You watch; the press will pick up on him!" one of the members stated.

"I wonder what his deal is. I question his concern for the young," Clem said thoughtfully, studying the man as he made his loud exit from the room.

Bob Thorstenson had walked toward the group of council members. "If you're thinking about Oblensky, I know him well. He left his wife with a couple kids, taking his fourteen-year-old—old enough to work, I guess. He went to the Interior, I heard. He lived briefly in Petersburg. Those Norwegians weren't interested in his methods. Always looking for a fight or trying to cover up some sleazy deal with an attack on others. They didn't throw him off the dock, but he got the message."

"But what connection would he have with the observers? Or the girl? It doesn't make sense," Harold said.

"Maybe he just wants to be noticed," someone suggested.

"Yeah," Lee Alverson added. "Maybe he wants a job. He could be the official meeting ender."

That also ended the speculation.

The atmosphere of the hotel lounge was busy. People milled about with various objectives, but the air of expected evening socializing was there, heightening the gala aura of the place.

Lee, Clem, Harold, and Jim walked slowly down the broad staircase leading from the second floor to the lobby below. "Dr. Alverson, how nice to see you," a young man exclaimed as he met Lee on his way up the staircase.

Harold raised his eyebrows in question.

"A researcher from the university," Lee explained.

Jim leaned toward a lady coming up the stairs waving a packet of papers. He reached out to take them from her. "That's all we need, more paper," he said, but laughed good-naturedly. She patted his arm and looked sympathetic. "Sorry," she murmured.

Clem looked for the source of the shouted greeting, "Hey, Red." He then saw a small, handsomely dressed Eskimo surrounded by a party of folks obviously engaged in a festive occasion. "Perry," Clem exclaimed joyously, waving his hand in greeting. At the bottom of the steps, he walked quickly across the room.

"He's from the Interior; fishes Bristol Bay," Jim said. "Clem knows them all. Where shall we sit?" he asked as they neared the tables outside the entrance of the dimly lit cocktail lounge. "Inside or here?" Jim asked.

"Out here," Lee responded. "I want to be able to see. As soon as Tillion gets through politicking, we'll get down to business."

"That might be a while," Harold observed, pointing toward Clem, who had gathered a crowd around him.

"He serves them well, and can't resist a chat," Jim said, grinning.

"He can't, or they can't?" Lee asked, smiling. "He'll get here. We'll order tea for him."

When Clem joined the group a few minutes later, they indicated to the empty chair in front of the pot of tea. "Is the tea for me?" Clem asked, sitting down. "Thanks. What's up?"

"Halibut," Lee replied.

Gordon Jensen, having heard the word "halibut," approached the table and sat down.

"Well?" Clem asked. "Derby system, or bycatch?"

"I think the bycatch figures are shocking," Harold said.

"They are," Lee replied, "but the system is in place. The cap is on bycatch."

"That's right," Harold said. "The cap doesn't leave anything for the fleet because the bycatch takes it."

"We can't do anything about that. The data show we can easily live with that," Lee replied.

"The fleet can't easily live with it. That comes out of their TAC [Total Allowable Catch]," Harold said bitterly.

Lee stared at him. "I know," he said. "And the long line fleet are the cleanest. It isn't fair. It isn't a good deal. However, we have to address reality here. Some system of individual responsibility must be devised to deal with the derby system in the halibut fishery and the bycatch. The increasing number of boats has turned the season into a bizarre race. Limited entry alone, as we have in salmon, wouldn't do it. The fishery is too different."

"Peter Pierce, in Canada, is advocating an individual quota system," Clem said. "I like Mark Lundston's version. I just hope those reviewing it see how vital it is. It's the old open-range, don't-fence-me-in debate. Times change."

"I think individual quotas are the way to go," Gordon stated.

Lee leaned far over, staring Gordon in the face. "Right, Gordon; you'd get half the quota for the North Pacific."

Gordon smiled. "You can say that, but it would work; it would be an incentive for a sensible fishery," he explained. "If it works, we haven't done a bad job. The other systems worked for a time, but there are simply too many fishermen and no regard for the biological damage in the mad race to get more and more."

Lee shook his head. "We have to examine every system before we decide."

"I have to agree with Gordon," Clem said. "It's the Tragedy of the Commons. We have outgrown that method. Let's determine on the side of the fish."

"Here, here," Lee said. "But I have some concerns for the old high-

liners from the Pacific Northwest who have tremendous investments. Just how one could structure it to not hurt them."

"I don't believe that any one man should have a right to own a portion of a natural resource that belongs to everyone," Harold said. "Besides, it just opens the door for huge companies to buy out all the quotas and eliminate the little fisherman."

Clem held up his hand. "I would have to protect my small boat fleet. They are the backbone of the economy for all the fishing ports and villages. No protection for them, no support from me."

A voice from the adjacent table burst into their conversation.

Gordon looked around and, turning back, said, "He was in the audience today."

"Boy, you guys," the man continued, "who the hell are you to be deciding what to do with a resource that belongs to us all? You look like a bunch of bureaucrats to me. What do you know about fishing—fishing from the fisherman's side of it?"

The room became quiet at the suggestion of a verbal battle.

"This is Dr. Lee Alverson from the University of Washington School of Fisheries, among other things," Clem said.

"This is Harold Lokken . . ." Jim started to say, but Harold butted in.

"We are all members of the North Pacific Fisheries Management Council, and we're trying to thumb through all possible solutions to what we call the 'derby system' of short seasons," Harold said in a placating voice.

"Oh, yeah, so you're the meeting going on upstairs," the man said. He was young, bearded and dressed like an outdoorsman.

"Are you a fisherman?" Harold asked.

"Salmon," was the reply.

"Did you like limited entry in salmon?" Clem asked.

"I wasn't here then, but I guess it was okay. But that's different; it didn't stop anyone from catching as many fish as possible. What you are talking about is stagnating," he qualified, "and a giveaway of the resource."

"If you aren't a halibut fisherman, how do you know so much?" Gordon asked.

"I have friends," the man said.

"I'm a halibut fisherman," Gordon stated. "Been one all my life. He fished halibut, too," he added, pointing to Clem.

Harold looked at the man kindly. "Testimony like yours will be heard. We are not making a decision; we're struggling with a problem.

61

This may or may not be the solution," he said. "If you have a solution, please come forward with it." Then Harold turned back to the table.

"Whatever solution is made will hurt someone. The solution we are living with right now drowns a few fishermen every year. That's not so hot either. We have to come up with something," Lee stated. He turned to Clem and Gordon, cutting off the young man at the next table, who also turned away, and, glancing at his partner, mumbled something and reached for his beer.

Lee Alverson shook his head. "I guess the party's over. We do have to have a chat and come to a consensus. What's the story for dinner?"

"I'm for Tempura Kitchen," Clem said.

"Not me," Gordon demurred.

"Give me an hour," Lee begged. "I need a little nap." He looked at his watch. "I'll meet you here at seven. Make a reservation." He stood up, picking up the papers, holding them in a posture of deep concentration as he made his way to the elevator. He felt so tired—tired of the uninformed, the misinformed, and the flat-out resistance to change. Those three things were so obstructive to making the best possible decision. It was like pushing an elephant through a knothole. Science was his life. Like his contemporaries he hated politics, but he knew that to be of service, the two were inseparable.

In the elevator, he leaned against the back wall, head back with eyes closed, thinking only of the pleasant sensation of the elevator moving upward. All too soon, it stopped. He leaned forward to step out, then saw the elevator had stopped for a man to enter. He glanced up at the numbers. Two floors to go. "It's going up," he informed the man.

The man who stepped in wore his heavy coat collar up, meeting the brim of his safari-type hat, and dark glasses hid the part of his face that could have been visible.

The man turned immediately toward the door opening, holding his gloved finger on the button marked HOLD. Inclining his head as if to look out into the hallway, he spoke in a high-pitched, muffled voice. "The death of the girl is not tolerable. You will make changes."

Lee was stunned. "What do you mean?" he asked. "What changes? Who do you think you're talking to?" he asked angrily.

"No girls," the man said. "I know who you are." Letting go of the HOLD button and pressing the CLOSE button, he stepped quickly from the elevator as the door closed and it continued upward.

On his floor, Lee quickly walked to his room thinking, *Good Lord. What did that mean? It wasn't that nut who testified at the meeting. Obviously it had to do with the observer. The thing was getting out of hand.*

But why would he corner me, and how would he know I was in the elevator?

He phoned Elmer Rasmuson. His wife, Mary Louise, answered. "I'm sorry; Elmer isn't home yet. I'll have him give you a call when he gets in."

Lee rubbed his chin. "Wardleigh," he said out loud. "He might have seen something." He ran down the number and called. "No; Tom hasn't come home yet," his wife, Jan, said. "Shall I have him call?"

"No; that's okay," Lee said, and then changed his mind. "Yes; have him call, please."

He called Clem's room. No answer, He left a message: "I'm going to skip dinner . . . have a snack here. I have some calls to make. [Signed,] Lee."

Clem had moved into the lounge. He was feeling deserted. He

wanted very much to go to Tempura Kitchen for dinner. Spotting Brad Matsen, the West Coast editor of the *National Fisherman's Magazine,* he waved.

Brad made his way across the room, greeting this one and that, his ever-present notepad in hand. He sat down at the small table, waving away a waitress who instantly appeared.

"How about dinner at Tempura?" Clem asked.

"Sure," Brad replied. "What do you make of the accident? And what about that Oblensky?" he asked.

Clem looked at Brad. He was tired of small talk. "I'll tell you over sushi," he said.

"The accident was unfortunate, and in some unknown way, Oblensky had access to the knowledge. He was prepared to make that speech before we'd read about it in the paper," Clem said, after having consumed three large sushi. "I think the accident was just that but I'm not sure where Oblensky is coming from. It's been made very clear that he isn't interested in the youth of America."

"Well, the word from the report is that the death was an accident. There was no evidence of foul play," Brad said. "I asked the authorities to advise me immediately because of the meeting. For those who would be most anxious."

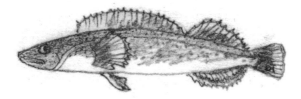

Three

Jim Branson, having been cut off by the young fisherman, sat silently watching. As executive director of the North Pacific Management Council, he was a professional listener. Now he leaned toward Harold Lokken and remarked, "I'm glad you flagged those bycatch figures. That's a bomb waiting to explode."

Bob Thorstenson nodded in agreement.

Harold replied, "It's a lot more complicated now than it was in the good old days when you were in charge of the Kodiak District and chased the foreign fleet and I was trying to establish a layup program to stabilize the market. That all seems penny ante now."

"Boarding those foreign vessels from the Coast Guard cutter was excitement and terror at the same time," Jim said. He leaned back in his chair, reaching for his glass, smiling with great satisfaction. "Yes, but the good old days were prior to statehood. I moved to Anchorage from Wrangell in 1951 and was learning to fly in 1952. You had to pay your own way then. The Fish and Wildlife Service didn't help you. But flying was the only way to go. The territory was so big. Tom Wardleigh gave me some instruction. He already knew about everything there is to know about flying."

"Ironically, that fellow, Oblensky, was one of our targets. He had his kid hunting and fishing. Ray Tremblay and I almost caught him up near Bethel," Branson said.

"Never mind him. What about boarding the foreign fleet?" Bob asked.

Branson looked around. The tables nearby had become quiet, and his expression changed to one of eagerness. He sat back and continued happily. "Interesting case in 1965; about the time you were setting up your cannery, Bob. I was in charge of the Kodiak-Aleutian Islands-Bering Sea District. We heard there were a couple Japanese ships off Norton Sound fishing herring. We flew up to take a look. There they were, two mother ships, and about fifty catcher boats. They had herring nets strung everywhere right from the beach and in the whole Sound. I called the Coast Guard. Did they have a plane? They said no, and their nearest boat was five days away. I called Anchorage. Did they have a plane?"

"We flew surveillance every day. One pass was very high, making sure they were still there while the Coast Guard cutter steamed north. The ship finally arrived at about 2:30 to 3:00 A.M. We were in the land of the midnight sun and, being June, it was bright as day. We put an agent on the Coast Guard cutter at Kothlik, then told the skipper to blast around the corner and we'd be flying overhead. They did, and had to shoot across the bow of one of the Japanese boats to make it stop. The other one got away. All the catcher boats cut their gear and ran for it, leaving gear in the water for miles.

"There was another ship, anchored off on the outside, around the point. We landed and taxied up to them and circled the ship with the plane. Finally a guy comes out and, seeing us, runs for the anchor gear. We fired across his bow, so he ran back inside and then Japanese began appearing all along the decks. That's the only ship I know of that was captured by an airplane.

"I told the Eskimos of Norton Sound that if they would clear the gear out of the water, they could have it, thinking that would be a real score for them. We took the offenders into Nome to court. Washington

called a halt to the Eskimos getting the gear. They let the Japanese come back and collect it. That was tough to explain.

"There were so many foreign ships out there. Japanese, Russian, Korean, and Taiwanese. Many of the fleet were so well organized that the Coast Guard had great difficulty making arrests in spite of their many violations of the twelve-mile limit. Coast Guard procedures that called for frequent radio contact and constant radar surveillance alerted foreign ships to their presence long before they could approach.

"For instance, one day I heard there were two just east of Amlia Island, in the Aleutians. Onboard the Coast Guard cutter, I requested they turn off the marine radio and radar systems and head for the Pribilof Islands. It took a bit of persuasion," he smiled a victorious smile, "but they did. We got well north in the Bering Sea, straight southwest of Atka, and came busting back out through Amutka.

"There they were—two Japanese trawlers within the three-mile zone. We dropped one boat and headed for one of them, while the cutter headed for the other. When I got aboard, some of the fish were still flopping. By the time the cutter stopped the other vessel, the fish were dead, so they couldn't prove they had been fished within the twelve-mile limit. The first went to court at Kodiak and a million-dollar fine was collected.

"One year we spotted a Russian ship—north, about fifty miles into the ice. We, on the Coast Guard ship, pushed our way through, but the fog was so thick you couldn't see. It was exciting, all right. Often damned nerve-wracking.

"That ship was a 600-foot crabber using tangle nets. We boarded

67

her. There were no violations, and we didn't understand each other, but we drank a lot and patted each other on the back. I still have a fur hat from that ship. That was the first Russian ship ever boarded off the United States by U.S. officials. We collected 7.1 million dollars in fines from foreign ships in 1975," he stated with a great sense of satisfaction.

"In that case, it doesn't sound like the Coast Guard did too bad of a job," Harold observed.

"Enough said of the old days," Jim said, waving his hand in a gesture of dismissal.

"I expect Gordon, here, has a few sea stories to tell," Branson said.

Gordon smiled, turning his head a little to one side, in a shy gesture. "Just fishing stories; not too interesting," Gordon replied.

They turned in unison when a man standing behind the table remarked, "Well, well, well, the old fudd's table. No wonder you can't address an immediate problem. All you can dream about are the good old days when you all felt *so* important in your fish hawk uniform. I heard you mention my name. You didn't care about the young then, either. They were hunting and fishing for their livelihood, not for sport." Oblensky stood over them, sneering. "Ah, yes, the purveyors of death to the young and innocent." He was not a tall man—perhaps five eleven—but his broad shoulders, long bull neck, and menacing posture made him appear a foot taller. He was so close they had to lean back in their chairs to see him.

Gordon Jensen rose. He rose slowly from his chair a little to the right of the intrusive figure. As his six-foot-seven frame continued to rise higher and higher, Oblensky became diminished. Gordon stood close to the man; Oblensky backed away, startled by the comparison.

He'd certainly seen Gordon in Petersburg many times and was familiar with his height, but the intervening years had increased his whole size. Gordon's expression was gently humorous as he remarked, "Nice to see you've learned about the needs of the young, but we know you, and we wonder what the scam is. I think you might want to go talk to someone as misinformed as yourself."

Oblensky stepped back. For just a second, envy for the group flooded his face, then was replaced with a flush of anger. He spun on his heels and walked out of the room, to the door, and out of the hotel. Someone at an adjacent table clapped. Gordon glanced at him, nodding slightly, and sat down.

"God, I wonder what he's up to," Branson remarked. "I think he bears watching. He must be damned old, but he's as crafty as ever."

"Well, if he is up to something, it will show up pretty soon. He's never been one to be subtle or silent," Bob Thorstenson observed. "What was the reference to the young folks?"

Jim Branson laughed. "Oh, that probably relates to an arrest. Actually, they were kids, so they just got a good scare. It was near Bethel. Upriver. Ray Tremblay and I caught them red-handed with out-of-season birds and a couple animals. His kid must have been one of the boys."

Bob Thorstenson shook his head. "Sounds like he's passing along his rotten attitude." Then turning to Harold Lokken, he changed the subject. "I'm interested in these figures you produced and in ordering a pizza."

"That sounds like a good idea," Gordon said, waving his arm at the waitress. After they had ordered, Harold Lokken laid the piece of paper with the figures on it on the table. "It's history repeating itself. They say it in different words, but it's the same."

The food came, and each man applied himself to the repast, retreating into the world of taste, relaxation, and private thoughts.

Bob, having started to think about the history of the fisheries, dropped the urge to talk about it with the arrival of the food, but continued the train of thought, remembering how it was after they did buy the cannery. When they'd purchased the cannery at Petersburg, only fifty-nine of the 147 canneries that had once bordered the coast of Alaska remained. Even the halibut seasons that everyone says are healthy were 117 days then, with a quota of 30.2 million pounds. The season this year was thirteen days with a 13 million pound quota.

When they bought that cannery, they had taken a terrible risk. Bob chuckled to himself as he recalled the panic of that beginning in the face of all odds. He glanced at Jim. *I guess that whole era of new beginnings was a time of panic,* he thought.

When the new company "Petersburg Fisheries" took over their purchase, it seemed simple enough. Bob Thorstenson remembered assuring his partners that, after all, he had been the accountant and knew all the details of operating the cannery. Bob thought of that now, remembering how he had choked out the "Roger; got you solid," after talking to the last tender. Placing the mike of the marine radio in its bracket, Bob pondered, *My God, what shall I do? What can I do? There will be more fish than the cannery crew can handle.*

Bob reached for the telephone. He'd call Gordon's wife, Helmi. "Helmi," he said, trying to sound calm, "Helmi, I have to have help. The tenders are coming in with more fish than the crew can handle. The

cannery crew can't possibly manage it. Who can I call for help? Who can just step in and do the job?"

Helmi did not answer for what seemed a long time. "Well, Bob, I think just about everyone can. You'll have to give them some warning, though. I can certainly help," she added. "I'll be right over."

"But who should I call to get in touch with everyone?" Bob asked, panic now clearly evident in his voice.

Helmi laughed. "Ask the fire marshall to ring the fire alarm," she advised.

The fire alarm sent the folks of Petersburg in a panic that brought them to the dock and then to meet the incoming fish. They dove into oilskins and gloves to work late into the night. Bob, like everyone else, had never worked so hard in his life. His years in the salmon cannery at Point Roberts stood him in good stead. He moved from one section to another, giving a hand here, some advice there, never pausing to rest.

At 4:15 A.M., a few stragglers still remained, putting finishing touches on the job. Three ladies scrubbing the cement floor moved slowly, from sheer exhaustion. One of them stopped and stood, leaning on the deck broom she had been pushing with one hand while holding a gushing hose in the other. The water was snaking its way to the trough that would take it out of the building. "I think we've about cleaned ourselves out of a job," she said. The other two came to stand beside her, giving their brooms a little push, as if reluctant to stop.

"It looks good," Bob said. "It looks great." He paused. He was not a demonstrative man. "Thank you," he said simply, with greater praise in his expression. They knew him and smiled. They knew. He watched them walk away in the dusky light, shaking his head. What great spirit they had.

The cook from the "Fiska Flicka" restaurant had closed his door to come add his skill with a knife on the slime line after he'd served dinner. Now, as the handful of men who were still putting things away clustered up, he said, "I'll cook breakfast if one of you guys will be the waitress."

Six men nestled down on chairs around the restaurant table. Bob was serving coffee, the scrambled eggs and bacon the cook was turning out as if by magic, as well as buttering toast as it popped out of the toaster. "By George, that was one sweet load of fish," one of the men said.

"Statehood sure turned the tide on the fishing scene," another mumbled through a mouthful of food. Then, taking a big swallow of coffee, he smiled blissfully at the others. It wasn't just fish. It was the jackpot.

"You mean Clarence Anderson?" Bob said. "He's the one who's had the brains and the guts to get a grip on the management system."

"Who's that?" another one asked.

Bob stared at the fellow, then shook his head. "You're hopeless, Pete. He's the new commissioner of fish and game. He's the fish boss. You'd better pay attention to these things."

"I heard the governor invited the Japanese in to buy fish and allowed investment in fish plants," Pete said, ignoring the remark.

"Pete pays attention when there's money involved. He just isn't interested in politics," his buddy explained.

"You guys going to go partners with them, too? I hear they're offering a good price," Pete continued.

Bob towered over them. He seemed to get taller as he formed his reply. "This cannery is going to be owned by Alaskan money. By the people who live here, and the fishermen who fish for it, and it will operate with U.S. dollars. That is our goal," he stated firmly.

"That will be a first in Alaska," a man named John said wryly.

"We may have to ask for time from our fishermen in order to match the Japanese price, but we'll do it!" Bob said with conviction.

"If we can make it without the Japanese, why can't the others?" a young man asked, puzzled. "I mean, it doesn't seem like anyone would choose to take foreign money, give to a foreign market."

"The fishermen did. They would not settle for the U.S. cannery price and the Japanese offered more, so they got the governor to OK it. But you have to remember, on the side of the U.S. companies, they were all trap canneries; statehood took those away. Right on top of that, the 1964 earthquake destroyed a lot of property, and in many cases, the government came in and bailed them out. I know in Seldovia they promised they would rebuild if they got the urban renewal money to recover, but the canneries took the money and ran. If you were in their shoes, it's hard to say what you'd do," Bob said. "They didn't have a Petersburg," he added proudly.

"Yeah, yeah, and those traps that were touted as being so 'clean' and 'environmental' took the salmon down fifty percent in just ten years. If you read Dick Cooley's book, *Politics and Conservation,* it'll knock your socks off!" an old-timer stated.

"Gee, Ole, I didn't know you knew how to read," one of them joked—a past victim of Ole's endless information.

John turned to Bob. "Thank goodness that loudmouth Oblensky wasn't here. He'd have fouled everything up. You'd never get him to donate his time."

"I always wondered what happened to him. I always suspected

there was some connection between him and the death of the China-man," Ole said.

"That's absurd. Oblensky was harmless, just a nuisance," Pete protested.

"Whatever did happen to him?" one of the others asked.

John leaned forward. "I ran into Norm Nilson in Seattle; you know, Portlock Smoked Salmon. Well, he was telling me about this wild guy, up on the Kuskokwim, that tried to sell them some salted kings he said were downriver fish. But you can't fool Norman; they were from way upriver, and of course they wouldn't buy them. The guy had a big temper fit. Norm just laughed. I guess he's used to tempera-mental fishermen. So, anyway, obviously Oblensky's up on the river fishing. Heard his kid went to law school, so he knows all the angles. He's . . ."

"Oh, God, John, who cares?" Pete groaned. "I'm going home to bed." They all stood up, eager to escape non-Petersburg trivia.

"Hey, we'd better tip the waitress," Ole said, digging in his pocket.

"Get outta here," Bob laughed.

When the next fishing period came, the town was ready. Merchants closed their doors. They put signs in their windows: "KEEP THE MONEY IN PETERSBURG." The banker closed all but one window, sending the rest of the people to the cannery. "I didn't take this job to be on a slime line!" one of the tellers objected.

The banker looked him in the eye. "This is money for our bank—money for Petersburg. It's inseparable. You can quit, of course," the banker replied.

The people who had worked before were the first to arrive. Helmi went directly to the packing line to sharpen her knife and claim her area. "You don't have to work this time, Helmi; there will be plenty of help," Bob protested. He'd seen her come into the cannery and walk swiftly toward the table where she'd stood before, packing bits of fish into the light cans, deftly slicing off the exact amount to complete the weight.

"Of course I have to work," she laughed. "I'm an old hand here. You need me."

Bob hardly heard the end of the sentence. He'd spotted a young man wrestling with a slimy fish that refused to stay put. Each time the man let go, it slid away and dropped to the floor. Bob dashed to his side, bending to pick it up and gently slipping it onto the wet table. "Here," he said, "take hold of it by the gills or by the tail and don't let go. You can turn it any which way and do whatever you need to do if you don't let go," he instructed.

73

"You mean I'm anchored to that damn slippery thing?" the fellow choked. "I don't even know what to do with this," he said, brandishing the long sharp knife.

Bob stepped back. He looked desperately around. "Helmi," he called, "come over here." He turned to the man and said, "I think you'd better go up to the can loft. You can surely put lids in the machine." Then he asked Helmi, "Could you take over here until I can find someone to relieve you?" Taking the knife from the young man's hand, Bob placed it on the table.

The fish lay perfectly still when it was released. The young man stared at it. "Damn thing," he mumbled, as he followed Bob away from the sliming table. He could hear Helmi chuckle.

"It was wonderful," Helmi said later. "I was on a slime line next to a gal I'd gone to school with. We hardly ever see each other, so the time just flew by with so much to talk about."

At the hotel table, Gordon leaned forward and asked, "You dreaming, Bob?"

"Yeah. I was remembering how wonderful Helmi was. Everyone was." Bob grinned. "Good old Petersburg. I don't think there are many towns that fine left. . . . Must be the Norwegian influence."

"Or the Icelandic," Gordon added.

At Tempura Kitchen, Brad was asking Clem what it was like in the early days of the king crab fishery. "It must have been grand then. Wild and free."

Clem laughed. "That was in the early fifties. That is, for the small boat fishermen. The big trawlers were there for some time before that. By the time it was over, about three billion pounds of king crab had been harvested from the North Pacific. It was wild and free, all right. It's bizarre to recall that we had a hard time selling our catch." One particular scene flooded his mind.

"What do you mean you can't take my crab?" Red Tillion gasped when the man at the crane refused to let him deliver.

"We can only take crab from guys who owe us money," the man choked out, seeing the anger rise in the expression of the red-haired fisherman standing below on the deck of his boat, the open hold revealing that it was full of huge king crab.

Red leaped for the ladder and rushed up. He glared at the man on the dock, then bolted for the office of the Whitney Fidalgo cannery. Inside, the manager stood up, terrified by the expression on the face of the approaching fisherman. He rushed forward to lock the bottom half of the Dutch door to the office. It had a small shelf used as a desk when the office paid the cannery workers, and effectively barred the office from the fishermen. "Honest," he said. "Honest, Red. They said we have to get our money back, so not to buy from anyone who doesn't owe money." The manager was holding out his hands as if to push Red away.

"What the hell is this? Last winter you said you were short on money, and I paid my bill. It took the last dime I had. Now you tell me I can't sell because I don't owe any. A hell of a lot of good that did me," Red screamed at the blanching countenance of the young manager. "What do you suggest I do with these crab?"

"I'm sorry, Red; I have orders. It does seem like a dirty trick."

Red spun on his heels and stomped back to the dock, grabbing a loose plank to beat on the lightpole, venting his extreme frustration on it while the dockman cowered in the warehouse. Heartsick, Red headed back up the bay to put the crab in his live box in Halibut Cove.

How was he going to make it if he couldn't sell the crab? It was a damn poor thing if a man was punished for paying his bills.

Unnoticed by him, a man stood in the shadows of the corner of the building and witnessed the whole scene. He was of medium height, with a trim, dark mustache; the leather jacket made him look the aviator that he was. He couldn't help but hear the fisherman's shriek of anguish and rebuttal to the cannery man. He walked out and looked at the name on the boat, then ducked back alongside the building as Red came charging back. He winced when the young fisherman beat on the lamppost, but empathized just the same. Elmer Rasmuson had flown to Seldovia that morning to visit with one of the cannery owners, Squeaky Anderson. That was the excuse since it was such a lovely day.

Elmer walked briskly to Squeaky's quarters and, after a brief greeting, asked, "Who's the fisherman with the Bainbridge?"

"You know him," Squeaky said, "It's Tillion. You loaned him the money for his place in Halibut Cove."

"Well, I just saw—rather, heard—him get turned down to sell his crab because he'd paid his bill," Elmer said. "Can that be?"

Squeaky shook his head. "Some operators are taking the philosophy that you have to keep your fishermen in debt to hold them, so they cater to those who don't pay. Right now there are more crab than they can sell. It's a tough deal all the way around," Squeaky said.

Upon hearing about it, fishermen friends went to the cannery manager, and made it clear that if that was going to be the policy, they wouldn't deliver and they'd see to it that no one delivered. They could deliver in Homer to Haltiner's outfit. Just because they sold salmon to that cannery didn't mean they had to sell crab.

"You can't scare me," the manager said, "but you can tell Tillion that the pressure's off and he can deliver now."

"Yeah, right; sounds like a reasonable deal. We'll tell him that." But Red switched to sell to Haltiner at Homer Spit.

In South Central Alaska there were many trap canneries, as in Southeast Alaska, as well as independent processors, like Squeaky Anderson and Port Chatham Packing Company, who bought from seine and gillnet fishermen, changing the scene of the fishery in the mid-fifties. They were exploring new methods and new grounds. Boats were pouring up the coast of Alaska, skimming the top of salmon runs in every area from Seattle northwest. While the halibut fleet out of Seattle was facing the increases in halibut boats from Alaskan ports, Alaskan fishermen were facing the increase of nonlocal salmon fishermen in their home waters.

King crab was becoming the new fishery. Clem Tillion, having es-

tablished himself in Halibut Cove with fishing boat and tiny house, settled in to study his new chosen field of fishing. He garnered data from the Smithsonian and from the Armed Services Institute about the fisheries, and focused on king crab, with studies from Japan and from Russia. Tom Wardleigh, who flew game wardens as well as the fisheries scientists, thundered into Halibut Cove in a big Grumman Goose, bringing new friends in the U.S. Fish and Wildlife Service who enjoyed exchanging information with that very knowledgeable, wild young man who knew things that surprised them. It was refreshing.

His neighbors did not reflect that, however. "Damn it, Red," they would complain. "You got the 'fish hawk' buzzing in here every other day."

Laying to off Homer Spit one day in his new boat, the *Donnie,* the weather too choppy to stay at the dock, Red was waiting for his deckhand who was due back in about an hour. He was drinking tea and listening to the marine radio. His attention sharpened when he heard the higher-pitched note of excitement as one crabber called another. "Hey, Joe, did you see that big trawler off Bluff Point?" Red reached for the mike. "The *Donnie* here. What's that you're saying about a trawler?"

"Yeah, I saw her dragging over by Bluff Point. I hope she got a load of coal. But it looked like she'd set a bunch of gear, too."

Another vessel broke in, "They sure did have gear—about a hundred pots! Gary says it's Wakefield."

"Well, that's the beginning of the end," Joe stated flatly. "I'm out."

"Hey, Red," Dick Haltiner yelled, running down the dock when he saw Red pull in to pick up his fishing partner. "Hey, wait a minute."

"I'll come in a little earlier tomorrow. I'm getting beaten up here," Red yelled to the man leaning over the edge of the dock.

"We have to stop this trawling in the bay. They'll wipe us out," Dick hollered back, urgency thick in his voice.

"See you tomorrow," Red shouted. Turning the bow line loose, Red dove into the cabin as the deckhand loosed the stern line and they pulled away from the dock.

The next day, Red arrived at eight o'clock. The seas were calm and he was ready for a long discussion. Dick Haltiner had seen him coming and was there when Red climbed up the ladder.

Red sat down on the timber along the edge of the dock, dejection written in his posture. A student of history, he knew this was the classic routine. It had been the story in every rich fishery, just like the salmon that was being decimated now.

Dick sat down beside him. "We can do it. We'll get a petition for everyone to sign, and present it to the Fish and Wildlife Service. If we all sign it, they can't ignore it."

"They certainly haven't been too concerned about the steady decline in salmon," Red stated bluntly.

"That's right, but this is a new fishery. There shouldn't be such an entrenched industry to defend it," Haltiner replied.

Red looked at him. He really believed they could.

"Okay; I'm game. You make the petition and I'll take it around."

"We can split the effort. I'll make two. You take one and I'll take the other, and we'll hit everyone."

Oscar Dyson wasn't about to sign. "I just rigged a trawl. I'm not going to sign that thing; you don't have any regard for those pioneering this business. Goddamn it, Red, I thought you were my friend."

"I am your friend, Oscar. There won't be any king crab fishery in Kachemak Bay for anyone to talk about if we continue to allow trawling. You're a drop in the bucket compared to what Wakefield is going to do here. The important thing is to protect this fishery for the local fishermen, for the local canneries."

"Goddamn it, Red, you're ruining everything," Oscar growled, and walked away with a "go away" gesture of the hand.

The petitions, presented at the next regional meeting of the Fish and Wildlife Service, were considered. To add drama to the concern, Squeaky Anderson stood up and testified for the crab. "I speak," he said, "for the female king crab. If I were to be caught in a pot, I would be thrown overboard to live. If I were to be caught in a trawler, I would be squashed and my legs, broken. There is no way that I would survive that. I beg you to protect me. Please do not allow trawl fishing for us king crab."

Everyone laughed at the comic figure he presented but took the testimony as much to heart as the petitions.

Trawling was banned in Kachemak Bay, although it was allowed to continue on the west side of Cook Inlet.

Heady with their success, the fishermen pushed for even more. "The next thing is to go after a pot limit in the bay. Ten pots can provide all the crab a fisherman can handle and the bay should be able to sustain," they proposed. Red and Joe Kurtz carried the request and that, too, became the rule. However, Wakefield continued to trawl for king crab on the west side of Cook Inlet. The 1955 total king crab poundage from there and other areas was 1,000,240 pounds. Other American fishing companies were rushing into king crab, and the Japanese were already well established in the Bering Sea. Restrictions in Kachemak Bay were a sop to a few local worrywarts.

Oscar Dyson moved to Kodiak where such restrictive attitudes were not taking place. However, within two years he was lobbying for no trawling around Kodiak, and was appointed to the Alaska State Board of Fish.

Dick Haltiner started test fishing with pots for shrimp with the few crab fishermen who fished for him and found it rich beyond expectation. Red fished for him and then began his own endeavor. "It was the classic shaggy dog story," he would say later. "We worked like slaves, went into debt that would take twenty years to survive, and got the royal shaft from a Seattle fish buyer. We processed twenty-three thousand pounds of shrimp that last winter, and when they canceled the last of the order, I was trying to peddle them on the streets of Anchorage. The markets weren't interested in the spiny things. I dumped a ton in the Homer Dump. Norman Nilson came to our rescue in Seattle, taking the shrimp out of cold storage and selling them for us. The other outfit said they were too fresh to sell, but they would take them off our hands if we paid the cold storage charges. In other words, get them all for free. It was the standard treatment of naive guys like me."

Dr. Norman Wilimovsky, head of the Fish and Wildlife Lab at Juneau, reported signs of serious depletion of king crab in Kachemak Bay just five years after the beginning of the fishery. A telegram came over the tiny marine radio, which served as the only communication in Halibut Cove with the outside world that Dr. Wilimovsky would be stopping by to talk about crab.

The big Grumman Goose roared to a standstill on the long beach adjacent to Red's yard. Three men came bustling up the path, meeting Red at the top of the beach. "Where's Tom?" Red asked, surprised not to see the pilot with them.

"He's down there," one of the fellows said, twisting his head around toward the beach. "I'm Norman Wilimovsky. I'm sure I know who you are."

Red took his hand and nodded but kept looking down the beach at the plane until he saw Tom emerge from below the bank. "What are you doing?" Red yelled.

Tom walked up to the foot of the trail. "Just whittling a few plugs here. Some SOB forgot to put the plugs back in the plane after the overhaul. Darn near sank coming in here," he said and walked back toward the plane.

Dr. Wilimovsky stared after him. "Looks like we were in luck with the pilot. We didn't notice anything unusual. He just held her hot and heavy to get to the beach without swamping."

Over tea, Dr. Wilimovsky said in an urgent voice, "We need to do a research program, collect some sort of database for this new fishery. I have proposed establishing a lab here in the bay—something basic from which to work. There will be a contract for the crab collection.

This must go out to bid, of course, but we thought you might be interested to throw your name in the hat."

Red nodded agreement. He would indeed.

The king crab research program in Kachemak Bay was insignificant to the intensification of the fishing effort for the crab. By 1966, king crab catches peaked. The total catch that year in the North Pacific was 160 million pounds, including U.S., Soviet, and Japanese efforts. Then it collapsed just a dozen years after the beginning. Dr. James Crutchfield of the University of Washington had voiced the following conclusion regarding Alaska salmon: "Until and unless it becomes possible to reduce the amount of gear to the minimum needed to take the permitted catch, economic waste, widespread violations of regulations, and a threat to the very existence of the industry will remain." History was repeating itself.

In 1961, the new Alaska Department of Fish and Game banned trawling in all state waters (up to twelve miles offshore) and extended area licensing for salmon to Prince William Sound. However, in spite of the fact that the Japanese had agreed at the International Pacific Halibut Commission meeting to back off and not fish halibut along the coast of North America east of 175 W longitude in 1952, this changed in 1963 in negotiations with the International North Pacific Fisheries Commission, allowing them to fish the Bering Sea. It was called "the

Bering Sea Giveaway." The Halibut Fishermen's Wives Organization in Seattle marched in protest.

Tom Wardleigh's visits with F.W.S. personnel increased in Halibut Cove. The conversations gathered more and more fire as the foreign fleet steadily increased. Red Tillion avidly absorbed the information and dispensed it to whomever would listen. Earl Hillstrand, a businessman from Anchorage and state legislator, built a large hotel at the end of Homer Spit. Named Land's End, it was a favorite stopping place for Red to have tea and talk fish. Earl and the representative from the Kenai Peninsula, Leo Rhode, were impressed.

On the day of the deadline for filing to run for office in 1962, Red got a message over his little marine radio. "Congratulations; you're running for office. Signed, Leo."

Leo, a highly respected man was expected to run again and had no contest to his Republican candidacy. He filed Red's name, Clem (Red) Tillion, handing Red a challenge with a minimum of struggle, in that he had no primary opponent. Of course, he had to win in the general. He had no car. No one even knew who he was, except the handful of locals that frequented Land's End Hotel on the end of Homer Spit and the members of the North Pacific Fisherman's Association for whom he often spoke, but Clem (Red) Tillion was running for election to the Alaska State House of Representatives, ready or not.

When Red received the message, he rushed out to his boat and motored across the bay to Homer's tiny harbor, then hiked the half mile to Land's End Hotel to tell Earl Hillstrand what Leo had done.

Earl was in the State House from Anchorage.

"Look at this," Red all but shouted at Earl, holding out the piece of paper he had scribbled the message on as it came over his tiny short-wave radio. "What in the world does Leo think. I don't even have a car!"

Earl shook his head, suppressing a smile. "I guess he thinks you can get a car and that you can win. I guess he wants you to put your money where your mouth is." Then he laughed, slapping Red on the shoulder. "Actually, you can ask him yourself here in about fifteen minutes. Have a cup of tea."

At the designated time, Leo and Elmer Rasmuson burst through the door, discussing a subject they were both very much involved in. Seeing Earl, they moved quickly to his side and included him in the conversation.

Leo was on the Board of Directors of Elmer's bank, and they both served on the Board of Regents for the University of Alaska.

Red, seldom at a loss for words, paled a little, wondering what he was going to say to Leo to express his appreciation for this confidence and wondering if he even had a slight chance to win the election.

The three men finished their discussion and, seeing Red, moved into the dining area and sat down at the table with him. Earl beckoned the waitress for coffee.

Leo's reply to Clem's inquiry was brief. "Of course you can win. We need someone who knows something about fish." Then, changing the subject completely, Leo turned to Elmer and asked, "Don't I remember that you were in Anchorage during the war? You know, I think people have already forgotten that Alaska was in the war."

"But, but how can you . . ." Red stuttered in vain.

"Yes," Elmer replied. "I came back to Alaska in 1943. We drove across country in April. We had Ed and Kyle then. She was just a baby. We went to Skagway first. When I saw how mistreated Skagway was during the war, I became an advocate of statehood right then and there. If I told you, you'd hardly believe it. When we got to Anchorage, it was quite another thing. General Buchner had a strong civilian attitude as well as a military one. It was a war zone in every sense, save the fighting. It was chaos. There was air raid practice, until the real one happened, and cars and trucks and buses were screaming out to Fort Richardson in the dark with no lights; civilians were diving for their prescribed shelters, and soldiers were so excited that some of them fired their guns while loading them. As it turned out, the Japanese plane that had been sighted heading for Anchorage ran out of fuel and crashed on Susitna Flats. The plane is at the air museum. The war contractors paid such high wages that it was difficult to get people to work in the bank. I worked as a teller and a loan officer at noon and late into the night every day. Sometimes we could get a soldier to work a little. They weren't supposed to work, but some of them would."

"Don't you think it strange that after the war the Japanese felt free to come into Bristol Bay to fish?" Leo commented.

"The fishery was the last thing on people's minds. The canneries and thirty-two-foot gillnet boats were mostly fished by outsiders brought up by the cannery from the outside, and the cannery was owned by outsiders. What the locals thought had little or no impact. It was the same in the rest of the coastal towns. A few locals made a living, but most of the money went outside," Elmer said.

Red scoffed, "It appears that the only notice by the Territorial Legislature was generated by rolls of dollar bills tossed through the hotel room transoms of influential legislators by lobbyists of the canned salmon industry."

"Yes, well," Elmer said, brushing aside the catty remark, "Alaskan bankers were pleasantly surprised when, after statehood, a far greater portion of that revenue was deposited in Alaska as the canneries and the fleets from local ports increased, and those Seattle fishermen fishing off our coast began to use the facilities available to deliver and provision."

Leo stood up. "We must go," he said. "Good luck," he said to Red, holding out his hand.

Red shook Leo's hand, flushing a little with emotion.

Elmer leaned across the table. "Good luck, young man; you'll need it. But if Squeaky Anderson and Leo, here, give you support, you already have a lot of it."

The campaign was a gentleman's campaign. His Democratic opponent was a family friend and a gentleman. The two men focused on issues and not personalities. The final tally was close. Clem had won by eleven votes, so there was to be a recount. The day that the recount was tallied, Red was driving to Kenai to attend a Masonic meeting. Hearing the news on the car radio, he went directly to his opponent's home, knowing they would both be at the meeting. They walked through the door together.

Allan Peterson had been the representative before Leo Rhode and was a well-known and highly respected man. As they walked through the door, Allan waved to the crowd inside. When they were quieted down, he announced, "Meet the new representative for the Kenai Peninsula, Clem Tillion."

Clem would be in a much stronger position to fight for wise management of the fisheries.

Four

The morning after the first day of the Council meeting, Jim Branson approached the table where Brad Matsen was having breakfast. "Clem tells me you were a stream guard in the Southeast," he stated, eyes shining with recall of his own early experience. "May I join you?"

"Well, Jim," Brad laughed, "you were the real quill. I'm afraid there's a big difference between your version and mine."

In 1963, Brad Matsen ventured to Alaska to seek a new frontier. Escaping his family, escaping the confined attitudes of Connecticut. He knew that if he were to make his own world, he would have to do just that—seek a new frontier. Alaska was as far as you could go.

Southeast Alaska was more spectacular than he could have imagined. Brad, and numerous other young men, applied for a stream guard job. Everyone from clean-cut, starry-eyed young fellows to seedy looking street sweepings stood in line hoping to be hired. He was assigned a post and a partner named Hank.

They left Auke Bay in a large Boston Whaler operated by a tough-looking Fish and Game man. They headed west toward Stephens Passage and then north-northwest up Saginaw Canal between Shelter Island and the northern tip of Admiralty Island. At Point Retreat, they swung around to head south along the west side of Admiralty for the approximate twenty-two more miles to their destination, Hawk Inlet.

The two young men eyed each other cautiously.

Brad was fair and quick, of medium height, and slender. Hank was a little taller, rather burly, and, at this moment, noncommittal of expression. They had both been relieved when they were chosen as partners, considering the many choices of young men, but now, as they left

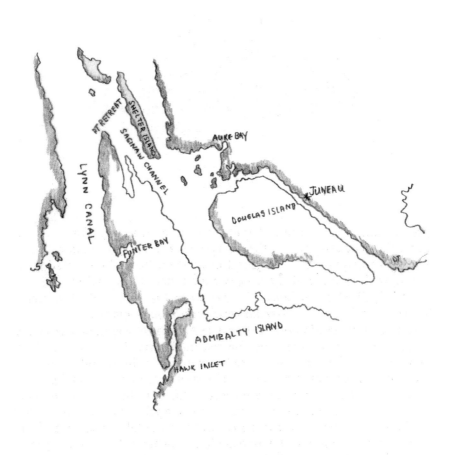

the brief training school, and the die was cast, with themselves as their only company for much of the summer, the reality of the decision settled like a cloak upon them.

Brad leaned toward the man at the wheel. "Do you make this run often?" he asked in a loud voice, as they sped along the strait's shoreline, pushed along by a northerly swell rolling down Lynn Canal.

The older man turned and leaned over as if he hadn't understood.

"Do you make this run often?" Brad shouted again.

"Nope," was the reply. "This whole stretch of water can be a weather hole," he added.

Brad looked back at the tiny skiff they were towing, their only means of transportation once he and Hank were dropped off.

The older man laughed, seeing the direction of the look and the expression of distress. "Hell, you guys will be in Hawk Inlet; it's plenty safe there. There's a sandbar at the mouth so the big seas can't push in. All you'll have to worry about are brown bears and creek robbers. But you got a gun there. You look like you can handle that. Hell, no problem." He laughed again, turning back to navigating Lynn Canal.

They passed Funter Bay, swinging a little clear of the rocks in the entrance. "Nice place, Funter Bay," the skipper yelled, but they could only see that there was a bay beyond the breakers.

There seemed no other break in the jagged shoreline that rose sharply to form what they both, now, knew was Robert Baron Peak and

Snowy Mountain. The trip seemed endless, but finally they made a right-angle turn into a narrow channel between jagged rocks. They were in Hawk Inlet. The sea was instantly calm. It was almost a shock to their senses as they cruised up the narrow channel to a tiny beach, where the skipper deftly landed and the boys pulled in the tow line of the skiff.

"There's a stream back toward the entrance. Good water, but you'll be better off here. The bears will be watching the stream for fish." They threw their gear over the bow of the Whaler. "You don't want to shoot one unless you have to," he shouted cheerfully, as he backed away from the beach, spun the boat around, and shot off downchannel without a backward glance.

Brad and Hank stared after the quickly diminishing black spot that was their last link to civilization. Brad turned toward the gear and began hauling it up the beach, not looking at his companion, not wanting him to see any sign of the distress he felt with that abandonment. Hank, grateful for the exclusion, grabbed a bundle of gear and headed for the top of the beach. An hour and a half of intense work with few remarks between them showed them that they could work well together. They chose a spot behind the lupin and the beach rye for their camp. They pulled the small skiff up into the grass so it would not be visible from the water.

When they were finished, exhaustion, and silence settled over them like a blessing. "My God, it's beautiful," Brad whispered, as if to himself.

"Yeah," Hank agreed. "No sense worrying about the bears. If they want us, they know where we are. They can smell us." He looked around. How could even a bear be mean in a place like this?

They hiked around, prepared a simple meal, then crawled into their sleeping bags. This was home. It wasn't all that bad.

They had pulled the skiff up into the grass. It had no motor. The instructions they had received were that if a creek robber was spotted, one man was to row out to the boat and arrest him while the other stood by with the gun from shore. The one boarding the vessel was to advise the crew that "a man with a gun is onshore ready to shoot."

They set up a bench rest for the gun.

Hank said, "Now, I'm no military man, but I sure can shoot; so if we ever see a creek robber, you row out and give him the authority treatment, and I'll keep a bead on him."

"I think you can row better than I can," Brad countered. "Why don't I man the gun?"

"Nope," Hank said firmly. "You definitely have a stern eye. Why, if

I went out there, he'd just laugh and say, 'Get outta here, you punk kid,' and throw me overboard. When you get serious, your eyes change color and get a real, not exactly mean, but firm look. They'll think you've got a six-gun in your belt."

Brad ducked his head modestly. "I think you're just afraid to row out there," he said. "But I'll go," he added.

They goofed around for days and days until finally the creek robber they were praying would never come, did.

It finally happened. They heard the boat long before they could see it. The northwest wind carried the sound of the motor up Hawk Inlet. The surge on their beach that swept up and back in a six-foot swathe revealed the magnitude of the storm outside. They rushed out beside the skiff and ducked down behind it out of the wind. The fishing boat motored slowly past. A man standing on the bow was clearly waiting for instruction to drop the anchor.

Hank and Brad followed them along the shore, staying out of sight in the forest. The boat anchored and one of the crew climbed up into the crow's nest, binoculars in hand, to scan the surface of the water for signs of fish.

"Go fix a sandwich," Brad ordered. "I'll keep the glasses on them." He never took his eyes off the fisherman who systematically turned from side to side until another man climbed up to relieve him.

The tide had changed and was going out as early evening light deepened the shadows.

Brad saw the raised arm, the excited leap from the crow's nest to the deck. The crew had swiftly pulled the anchor and they sped toward the mouth of Hawk Inlet.

Brad and Hank rushed toward the skiff. "We can't do anything until they set," Brad warned. They didn't have to wait long. The wind carried the command, "Let'er go!" and the boat spun into action.

Hank and Brad pushed the skiff down the beach. They reached the water at its ebb and Hank yelled, "Get in; I'll push you out when the water comes back." Brad leaped into the boat. The water didn't come up quite far enough. Brad leaped back out again and he and Hank pushed the skiff out farther. He leaped in again as the water started in. One of the oars fell overboard. Hank ran after it, wading to his waist. Brad placed the oars in the oar locks and, taking a mighty thrust, started the skiff moving smoothly out into the channel.

Brad turned into the wind. It was much stronger out on the water. He pushed with all his strength. "Did Hank have the gun ready?" he wondered.

The seiner was now beginning to brail the fish aboard. Brad wished he had the gun.

Head down, Brad rowed harder until he thought his heart would burst. When he looked up again, the fishing boat was headed for the entrance, already beginning to buck the swell.

Brad sat still, breathing deeply. The tide that should have swept him toward the fishing boat was now beginning to grab him; he rowed hard to get close to shore in the backwash in order to get back to camp.

He was too tired to talk about it.

That was the only fishing boat that came into Hawk Inlet. Eventually, they were happy to be moved to Point Couverden, where they did finally catch two creek robbers—a seiner they were glad to catch, and a couple of Indian kids in a big skiff that they were not.

"I don't think this is my cup of tea," Brad said, when the season was over, "in spite of my authoritative look," he added, and punched Hank on the shoulder.

Brad Matsen smiled at Jim Branson. "No; you wouldn't like to hear about my adventures as a stream guard," Brad reflected. "It was definitely hit-and-miss and then we got a couple kids. Indian kids with a big skiff."

That was such a long time ago, and yet it was just as vivid in Brad's mind as if it happened yesterday. "I don't think the fines they had to pay meant anything to the fishermen. It did to those kids, of course, but to the real seiners, it was chicken feed. Paying a fine was just part of the expenses, like fuel."

Jim Branson leaned back in his chair and scoffed, "You're right; they can talk all they want about fines. In Kodiak, Commissioner Ana Mae Vokachek found that three weeks in jail curbed more creek robbing than did fines."

"So, is that when you decided to become a journalist?" Jim asked.

"Oh, no, I decided to be a pilot then. Joined the Marines. Got washed out of flight school with rheumatic fever. I did learn to fly, though. I have a private license."

"And?" Jim persisted.

"I went back to school," Brad said, his expression clearly indicating that he was through even thinking about himself.

Brad stood up to leave. Branson, reluctant to give up, waved his arm in a sweeping gesture. "Here come Harold and Lee; have another cup of coffee. Actually," he said, in a confiding tone of voice, "I'd like to bounce something off your brain box."

Harold Lokken and Lee Alverson pulled out chairs to sit down at Brad's table.

"Tell me what you think of this," Jim said, leaning forward. "When I went home last night, I found a strange wire setup on my mailbox. I suppose some kid might have been playing a game, but somehow it didn't look like that."

Brad's head turned sharply. "How was it attached to the mailbox?" he asked.

Jim explained, using a sugar bowl as an example of the mailbox.

"Looks to me like it was wired to detonate," Brad stated bluntly; his eyes fierce with the realization. "You make somebody mad?"

"Now, how would you think that, from such a loose description? That's a bit reactionary, don't you think?" Jim asked.

Brad leaned close to Jim. "I worked for the CIA after four years in the Corps. That's what I went to school for. I worked for them for several years in Europe—all over Europe, in the electronic-technical section. Was there anything else besides the wire?" he asked.

Jim Branson laughed self-consciously. "Just a note in the mailbox that said 'No more girls.'"

Lee Alverson gasped and started to speak but changed his mind. He relaxed back into his chair to watch and listen.

"It's the observer thing," Harold mumbled. "This has gone too far.

We need to have a quiet investigation of the whole thing. Of that ship and of Oblensky, although surely he's only capable of being a pawn." He turned to Jim and said with a twinkle, "Thought your girlfriend had the goods on you, eh?" In spite of himself, Jim blushed.

Lee studied the room quickly filling with persons involved in the fisheries. He'd withhold his story until later. He'd talked to Elmer about it, about the man in the elevator. "We can't jump to conclusions," was Elmer's response. Lee readjusted his chair. "Let's talk about fish for a change," he said.

Clem Tillion appeared as if by the magic of the word. He sat down at the table.

"Yes, let's talk about bycatch," Harold added. "My flcet is not ignoring those bycatch figures. There has to be a way to put a cap on it far below the astronomical amounts now taken. INPFC figures show 4,597 metric tons from the foreign and joint venture fleet, and that doesn't include the U.S. numbers."

"The scientists say the stocks can handle it," Jim pointed out. He turned to Lee. "You're a scientist. Can the stocks survive that?"

Lee qualified, "That's what the Halibut Commission says."

"I'm asking you," Jim said bluntly.

"I don't know. I haven't studied the data. On the surface, it does seem unreasonable. I can understand your concern, but as a scientist, I'd have to review all the information to make a qualified statement. Those that do are supposed to know their business."

"Do you think the observers are qualified to make the judgments they have to make about the species and the poundage?" Brad asked.

"Yes," Lee replied. "I don't question that. They are thoroughly screened."

"Let's start pushing for individual transferable quotas; you know, ITQs," Clem suggested. Changing the subject, Clem stated, "It will take so long to get through the paper mill. We should start now. The steady increase in the fleet makes it imperative that we do something if we are to manage the fishery. At best, it will take four years."

"It's going to take longer than that," Harold said, shaking his head. "We'll have to do a lot of talking to even get it off the ground. I have to say, I do not believe in anyone owning a portion of a resource that belongs to the public, but I don't see any system that would work better. The majority of the fishermen will oppose it only on the grounds of the division of the spoils. The issues of the derby system, the marketplace, or the consumer will not be considered."

Clem scoffed, "The public have violated their rights all around the world. Only that which he owns does he take care of."

Lee leaned back in his chair. "A callous statement, Tillion. I suspect you're right, but science can't make those value judgments; it has to determine opinion on data from numbers." He looked at his watch. "I'll be right back; I have to make a phone call." He stood up and walked quickly to the row of phones against the far wall.

Lee eagerly waited for Elmer's response to his report of Branson's mailbox incident and note. Elmer was silent for a long moment. "Did you tell them about the man in the elevator?" he asked.

"No," Lee replied. "No; I didn't. I wasn't ready to get involved. It all seems so weird. So theatrical. The girl's death has been proved an accident, it seems that should be the end of it."

"It does that," Elmer said in a thoughtful voice. "Did they have an investigation?"

"Yes," Lee replied. "There was no evidence to indicate that it was not an accident. The Russian captain, Petrof, was very dramatic in the defense of his ship. He said the girl was young, as if that explained anything. I don't think it explains Oblensky's behavior or Branson's experience. There's definitely something fishy here. And I don't mean cod."

"Perhaps you should all come to our house for dinner and we can discuss it in more comfortable surroundings. Find out what you can about Oblensky. He's obviously a key, or a red herring. He isn't subtle or devious in his approach. Find out what possible connection he might have to the observer program."

After Lee hung up the phone, he dialed again. This time, to the Wardleigh residence. Tom answered. "Can you come over to the Hilton for coffee? This observer thing is thicker than it looks. Brad Matsen checked the report on the girl's death. It was an accident. The Coast Guard flew out there with the authorities, and it seemed quite straightforward. I've had a warning, if that's what it could be called; and now, today, so has Branson. I wonder if you saw anything that might suggest why this man Oblensky is so adamant about female observers."

There was a long pause before Tom Wardleigh replied. "I have someone here who might shed some light on the subject. Captain Vincent is here. He has a week off before returning to the ship. We'll be right over."

Lee Alverson returned to the table. "I think we're going to get some answers. Wardleigh is coming over, and he's bringing the captain."

"The captain of the ship? Where's the ship tied up?" Branson asked, surprised.

"It isn't. He's the American. It's a joint venture. There's a Russian captain aboard also," Alverson explained. "We'll get all the details when they get here."

Tension surrounding the three acted as a magnet to their usual group. Gordon Jensen and Harold Lokken came by, pulling a table and chairs closer to join them. A waitress arrived immediately. They didn't have to wait long before Tom Wardleigh was striding into the restaurant, followed closely by Captain Vincent.

After they were introduced and seated, Tom Wardleigh pulled the rumpled piece of paper from his pocket and placed it on the table. "This was on the top bunk of the girl's stateroom. It was obviously discarded. There was a young man on the ship of Russian descent. His name was Oblensky. The note, you will see, is addressed to him."

Jim Branson turned to Captain Vincent. "What is your idea about this? Were you aware of any sort of relationship between them?"

The young captain looked from one to the other. His answer would be critical. "I'm sure they were friends. They were, in many ways, alike—reserved and conscientious. The fellow's name is Ralph. Ralph Oblensky. I called his father in Juneau, and he told me that your man is Ralph's grandfather. He said his father was rather short-tempered."

"Was she unfriendly?" Brad asked.

"No. She was always busy. She kept very good records. Very thorough," the captain said.

"Do you think that young Oblensky was in communication with his grandfather?" Brad asked.

Captain Vincent rubbed his chin in a thoughtful gesture. "I don't know. Not to my knowledge, but a lot of messages were received—many that came to Captain Petrof in Russian or Polish, and others that were in English and Korean about the fish received by Mr. Cho. Since I couldn't interpret them, I didn't pay attention to that. My job was to navigate."

"Did the girl speak Russian?" Jim asked.

"Yes; yes she did. Very well, I might add."

"Do you think Ralph Oblensky could have been an agent for his grandfather?" Brad asked.

"I'm not sure what you mean. An agent for what?" the captain asked.

"I'm not sure. Why do you think old Oblensky might be fanatically against women observers? What possible connection could he have with the ship or his grandson? What possible activity could be taking place?" Brad pressed on.

"All our orders come from the office in Seattle. They work with the joint venture people and set the whole thing up," Captain Vincent said. "The messages are, as far as I can tell, communications with the buyers and to those foreign members of the crew."

Brad picked up the note from the table. "We still don't know what 'it' is. Mind if I have a copy made of this?" he asked Tom Wardleigh.

When Brad left the table to look for a copy machine, the others sighed. Sitting back in their chairs, they asked personal questions of Wardleigh, congratulated him on his reported aviator skill, and inquired about life on a factory ship from the captain.

When Brad returned, handing Tom Wardleigh the note, they all stood and said their good-byes before climbing the stairs to the meeting room, where they would become totally absorbed in the business of fish until it was time to accept their dinner engagement with Elmer.

The group that arrived at the Rasmuson mansion the next evening included Lee Alverson, Jim Branson, Brad Matsen, Clem Tillion, Bob Thorstenson, Gordon Jensen, and Harold Lokken.

Elmer and Mary Louise Rasmuson greeted their guests cordially. The seven men filled the spacious entry with an overwhelming degree of male energy. Mary Louise, dwarfed by them all, moved quickly to help Elmer take their wraps and then to lead everyone into the library for cocktails. After he had served them from the small bar, Elmer addressed Lee. "Well, what did you find out about Oblensky?"

Lee set his glass on the coffee table. "He lives at Bethel. He has one of those state jobs—economic development, I think, or some such division. It would be easy to check the record in Juneau. Although he is canny—so I think he would keep the record clean; but checking might reveal something, like who he favors or just how he operates."

"I can check that out," Clem offered.

"We met with Tom Wardleigh just after I talked to you. He had the American captain of the ship with him, but we didn't learn anything except that Oblensky's grandson, Ralph, works on the ship and was somehow involved with the girl," Lee Alverson said.

Brad pulled the copy of the note from his pocket. Handing it to Elmer, he said, "That's a copy of the note Wardleigh found in the girl's stateroom."

Elmer looked at the note. "Well," he said, "it does look like there's something going on," and handed it back.

"The captain was quite positive that the young Oblensky was not a chip off the old man's block," Harold said. "Said he was a quiet man."

Elmer pursed his lips and mumbled, "Ah, yes, a quiet man."

"The captain said their orders all came from Seattle. From the office," Lee added. "He did say that many messages came in Russian and that the girl spoke the language well."

"I can inquire around Seattle for some Russian agency or some such organization if you think he's that much of an operator. He seems crude, but he is articulate," Lee said.

"Well, he can't control his feelings, so I doubt that any international company would have him," Harold stated bluntly, his distaste for the man clearly written in his expression.

"I'll check around just the same," Lee mumbled.

"Personally, I find the man despicable, but might the job be too risky for a girl?" Gordon asked. "It's an unforgiving world out there, and a small miscalculation can be fatal. Girls aren't as crazy as boys are—I mean, about taking risks."

"I think the average agility between the sexes is about the same. There are a lot of accidents on those vessels. Whoever takes the job takes the risk. They know that when they sign up," Lee answered.

"I guess I wouldn't want my daughter out there," Gordon said.

Elmer turned to Harold. "I understand that Oblensky was part of your fleet in Seattle at one time. Do you think him capable of intricate intrigue?"

Harold looked out the window, his face blank of revealing expression. Then, turning to Elmer, he said, "I haven't witnessed any social grace, but he fished with the same man for years, and gained his respect and affection, so I guess I have to retract my earlier statement. If it is to his benefit, he can be any way he wants."

"I think we've exhausted the subject," Elmer said in a louder, more cheerful voice. "Let's talk about fish."

"I didn't realize you were involved. How did you get into the fisheries business, Elmer? It's very obvious why the rest of us are," Brad said, making a sweeping gesture toward the guests around the table.

"But I am," Elmer replied. "Or, I should say, my bank is. I felt I had to learn about the needs of the fisheries to understand the financial needs of it.

This huge fishery sneaked up on us. Alaskans were so used to see-

ing the foreign fleet out there off Bristol Bay and in the Gulf of Alaska, and were complaining about it bitterly. We didn't shift gears when they were under control, and the problems were generated by our own vessels. The imagery of the local fisherman was some dumb guy with a leaky boat barely eking out a living. So, when fishermen started coming to the bank for money, the instinct was to say no. Then I knew it was time to start learning about the fisheries.

"The International North Pacific Fisheries Commission provided the first rational management of the fisheries of the North Pacific, and I was privileged to have been appointed to that commission. I believe that my coming onto INPFC changed the attitude toward the scientific group.

When I was chairman, we set a policy that all decisions would be determined from the information given to the commission by the scientific committee. This gave that committee a standing it hadn't had, and the scientists of Japan, Canada, and the United States worked closely together to provide the commission with the sound data from which the decisions were made. It put the scientists in a unified position instead of the politely combative position of the negotiators for each country."

Brad had listened attentively. "I was aware of your role as chairman of the North Pacific Fishery Management Council, but I guess it escaped me that you had come from such a role on INPFC."

Elmer smiled. "Most of my life, I have come into a situation of trouble, and the council was the single exception. It was a pleasure. The reason the North Pacific Management Council has done so much better than all the other councils around the United States is because the basic members of it came directly over from INPFC and knew about fish, and also already had a policy basis for their actions."

"Speaking of management," Harold said bitterly, "we'd better address this bycatch issue. I find it ironic that they use the term 'incidental' in the data. It sounds so trivial."

Gordon leaned back in his chair. "Isn't that the truth," he scoffed. "That 4597 metric ton figure represents over ten million pounds thrown overboard, supposedly," he added.

"If Lee, here, is right and the observers do a good job, 'supposedly' should not be a factor," Jim pointed out.

Gordon leaned forward to address Jim, sitting directly across the table, "I can't believe that those foreign ships in the joint ventures actually dump all the high-priced fish, like halibut, overboard. On INPFC, I listened to the Japanese. They're crafty devils, and we have a few on our own side who can figure. The guy who gets hurt is the clean fisherman in the long line fleet whose quota is diminished and whose market is invaded." Gordon's voice was soft but vehement. The other men at the table remained silent for a long minute.

"There isn't any question that the problem must be addressed," Harold repeated firmly.

"It's the same story since history began. By the time anyone notices or cares that there's a danger of overexploitation, the dollars involved provide a lobby. INPFC addressed the foreign fleet; now the council must address the U.S. fleet and the new joint venture thing," Elmer stated. "There is nothing static about the industry."

"We have to go individual, transferable quotas," Clem said. "It has been successful in Canada, and is the only thing that can save the fish."

"That doesn't affect the trawl fleet," Brad reminded him.

"I mean we should have ITQ in all the fisheries. If those trawlers knew they weren't racing every other trawler for a share of the quota, they'd have an incentive to be conservative. As it is, they're pressured by time and by the ever-increasing number of vessels out to get their million before the whole thing collapses. The day of the open range is over. I'm not saying that the ITQ system is the only way it can be done, but I haven't seen another suggestion that is better," Clem added.

"What about limited entry? That has worked fairly well for salmon," Bob asked.

"It would not eliminate the race. There are too many vessels that must stop fishing as soon as the quota is reached," Clem replied.

"It would be a change for the processors," Gordon pointed out. "The fishermen would have time to seek other markets. The processors would have to catch as catch can for product."

"Thanks, Gordon," Bob said. "Few people look at things from the processors' side."

"There will be changes for the fishermen, too," Clem added. "They won't be able to sell a third-rate fish. Quality will be the leading factor. This is happening worldwide. Our derby system has blinded the fleet to that fact. They will have to take the time to learn the skill of handling the fish to produce a first-rate product. When you visit the fish markets in Japan or those in Denmark, you can hardly bear the way we throw our fish around and sell it third rate."

"They also won't get caught out there with a deckload when a storm blows up and swamps them," Gordon added. "That almost happened to me in 1965. I still had the *Symphony*. She was just fifty-seven feet long. We were fishing up Seward Gulley. Had a real fast trip in the spring. The boat was full of fish, had fish on deck. We got caught in a blow, and a comber came over the stern and went all the way to the pilothouse. I just stood there and looked to see if the stern was going to come back or not. It did. As soon as I got to town, I called Berg down at Blaine and said, 'Start building.' That was the beginning of the boat *Westerly*."

The men at the table were silent, looking at Gordon, and then at their plates, imagining themselves standing inside a fifty-seven-foot boat—My God, it was fifty-seven feet from the kitchen to Elmer's library—watching the stern disappear under the oncoming swell that had followed a succession of combers building higher and higher. Each one looking like it would come over, but the heavily laden vessel would tip and lift each time, leaving a brief wake of relief, a deep breath, and a prayer of thanks. Then came the one that loomed high above the stern long before it reached the vessel, leaving no question of the outcome when it did. Each man had his own version of that horror-stricken moment that makes time stand still.

Gordon, joining the silent chorus of imagery, felt his stomach contract as he again saw that wall of water advance, blocking the horizon of the great North Pacific. That ocean swell rising higher and higher, changing color from dark, menacing blue-gray, to a pale green shade filled with light just before it broke over the stern and became a crushing, tumbling blanket of tons of water pressing the already laden vessel down. Gordon shook his head and cleared his throat. "Well," he said, with a wry grin, "it was time for a bigger boat. We all take crazy chances."

"I think we can all say that," Elmer agreed.

They all looked at him in surprise. Elmer, the banker?

"Of course," Elmer said, as if reading their minds. "I haven't spent my whole life behind a desk."

Lee smiled. "I'll testify to that. Actually, Gordon's tale most clearly demonstrates the need for ITQs. That is the scene every year; without a happy ending."

"As you know," Harold Lokken said, "I don't philosophically agree with the concept of the private ownership of a public resource, but it seems to be the only way and is just another dramatic change in the fisheries. All of us here, except perhaps Brad, who is too young, albeit knowledgeable, have watched a succession of changes in the fishery. At first, we were all concerned about the foreign fleets in the North Pacific and Bering Sea. The passage of the Magnuson Act in 1976 brought that under control, but unfortunately a U.S. fleet would supplant it with ever more vessels aided by the electronic age, which has changed the whole concept of fishing. The old halibut fleet was child's play in comparison with their electronic devices and equipment designed to literally sweep the ocean clean of every living thing. The investment in these vessels gives the companies a lobby in Washington, just as the salmon industry had in the trap years. That it has happened so quickly is shocking. In three generations, to see fishing expand in the vast North Pacific and Bering Sea to the point of needing ITQs, to a season limited to hours. To see companies invest millions, racing to catch even more millions' worth of product, gambling that it will last long enough to pay off. It is truly no different than the gold rush to California. The bycatch waste is a result of that panic of greed. A tragic result," Harold said, shaking his head.

Clem put up his hand in a "halt" gesture. "But ITQs are just another tool toward management—like limited entry in salmon, or the extension of jurisdiction, or the sound management the Halibut Commission has exerted over that fishery's stocks. Times change; they always change, so adjustments have to be made."

Gordon chuckled. "No one likes change, or necessarily sees that there is a need. You should hear what my son thinks I need to change on my boat."

They all laughed, equal victims of the generation gap.

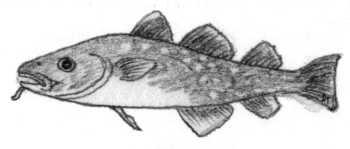

Five

Brad Matsen collapsed into a window seat of the aircraft; found and fastened the seat belt; leaned down to pull his briefcase closer to his feet from where he had tossed it, placing it within easy reach, then relaxed. Staring out of the tiny window, he watched the crew throwing luggage and freight onto the conveyor belt that would carry it into the body of the plane. He sighed heavily. He was tired.

During the North Pacific Fishery Management Council meeting, each of the factions regarding changes in the regulations had presented their version of a management plan, knowing that he would be writing an editorial for the *National Fisherman's Magazine* on the meeting. He had to listen carefully. Had to set aside his own opinion for the moment to be sure he hadn't missed a point. He turned to the magazine in the seat pouch and thumbed through it, studying the maps of the United States in the middle. He was thinking of a trip out East later in the year. He scanned the articles designed to entertain travelers. It was so relaxing to just let the pages speak. The plane backed away from the terminal and taxied slowly. Brad watched the scene change as they moved along, enjoying even this aspect of flying. Soon the plane had turned and started down the runway, steadily increasing power, then lifting off and banking toward Turnagain Arm and Prince William Sound. He pulled his briefcase onto his lap. He looked over the data sheets from the meeting. A stewardess came with a menu; he ordered, pulled down the tray for the vacant seat beside him, and continued to read. When the food came, he picked at it while still reading.

Suddenly, he stopped chewing. "That voice," he thought. "I know that voice." He listened intently. It was that man Oblensky. The sound was faint, so he had to be far back in the plane. Brad wished he could hear what Oblensky was saying, see who he was talking to.

A stewardess came by with a cart to remove the dinner trays. A second followed with fresh coffee. She stood for a moment in the doorway of the first-class area. Through the opening of the curtain, Brad was sure he saw Lee Alverson. When the dinner hour was over, he stood up, carrying his briefcase, facing the front of the plane as he moved out from the window seat.

"Brad," Lee exclaimed, "I didn't see you in the terminal." He looked around. The seat across the aisle was empty. "You can sit over there and we can talk," he said.

Brad sat down and, leaning across the aisle, said as quietly as he could, "Oblensky is on the plane."

"Did he see you?" Lee asked.

"I don't know, but I don't think so," Brad said. "I wish I could see who he was talking to. Although I dare say he would be talking to anyone that would listen." Just then, a stewardess stepped through the curtain. Brad ducked out of the way.

"You can't sit here without a first-class ticket, sir. Sorry," she said.

"All right. I just had a message for Dr. Alverson, here," Brad explained, hoping the title would impress her.

She turned toward Lee as if to speak to him, then changed her mind and turned back to Brad. "Sorry," she said firmly.

"Try not to let him see you when we get off," Brad said to Lee as he was leaving. He held his face down, looking into his briefcase as he made his way back to his seat. He longed to stand tall and locate Oblensky.

At the Seattle airport, Brad moved over to the aisle seat, placed his briefcase in the middle seat, and made himself busy with it, his back to the aisle and his ears straining to hear some sound that would indicate Oblensky's passing. It seemed an eternity as people slowly moved along, waiting for some to get things from the overhead rack, or put on their coats and gather things placed under the forward seat. Just when he was sure he'd missed Oblensky, Brad heard his voice again.

"It's always the same," Oblensky said. "It takes almost as long to get out of the plane as it does to fly down here." Several people laughed a little.

Brad stood up when he had a buffer of five passengers. As he entered first class, he saw that Lee had already disembarked. He hurried up the causeway, pausing to look in all directions, before he entered the terminal. The passengers were moving rapidly toward the baggage claim exit. Where was Lee? Damn. He didn't want to head out after Oblensky without him, but he hurried on.

"Let's go," Lee said, right behind Brad. They rushed after the mob. "Where did you get that hat?" Brad asked, looking at the vari-colored wool cap Lee was wearing. "I didn't recognize you."

"It's my ski cap. Ruby knitted it for me years ago. Had it in my pocket. Thought I might need it in Anchorage. A bit of a disguise, don't you think?" Brad smiled. "Well, it isn't the expected attire for a council meeting."

"By the way, did you see the fellow who was with Oblensky?" Lee asked. "It was the man in the elevator; I'm sure. Same hat, same coat, same voice. It really knocked me for a loop."

"There they are, slow down," Brad said, holding out his arm to block Lee's path. They had turned into the luggage carousel area.

"Do you have luggage?" Lee asked. "I don't; I just have this carry-on," he said, indicating the bag he carried over his shoulder.

"Yes. I do, but if they don't or if it's a problem, I can get it later," Brad said.

"Son Bob's going to meet me," Lee said. "Do you have a car?"

"Yes; I do, but I think we'd better stick together. Will Bob be on time? That's critical."

"Yes; he will," Lee said. "In fact, there he is over there by our flight's luggage track. Oblensky is alone now. His companion must have gone for a car."

Bob walked swiftly over to Brad and his father. "What's the deal with the hat, Dad?" he asked.

106

"Never mind the hat," Lee said. "We want to follow that man, the one over there in the brown coat, and his companion, who must have gone for a vehicle. Right now, you and I will go sit in your car while Brad waits here to keep his eye on Oblensky and maybe even to get his own luggage. Come on." The automatic door of the terminal opened for them, and there, right across the sidewalk, was the car waiting for Oblensky. Lee grabbed Bob's arm and turning his head away, walked swiftly down the sidewalk.

"Slow down, Dad. My car's right here," Bob said. He pulled Lee back, opening the door for him to get in. "I'll put your bag in the trunk." Bob took the bag from Lee's hand and slammed the door shut as soon as Lee was seated. "So, what's the deal?" Bob asked, as he got into the driver's side. Lee explained about Oblensky's speech at the council meeting and about the man in the elevator, who he was sure was sitting in the car behind them, with just one vehicle as a buffer. Lee looked nervously into the rearview mirror frequently.

"We probably should drive around and get behind him," Bob suggested.

"No, no, we can't do that. We can't risk his driving away," Lee objected.

They didn't have long to wait. Oblensky emerged from the building laden with their luggage. The driver jumped out and opened the trunk. Oblensky handed him a bag, his expression angry.

"I thought Petrof was going to be on this flight. He said he'd meet me here to square things with me!" Oblensky blurted out. "What does he think I am? Just a puppet?"

The other man was placing the luggage in the trunk of the car. "Perhaps he's already here," the driver said in a placating voice.

"I didn't like his attitude about that stupid observer. He wouldn't give me any support to get rid of the damn pests," Oblensky snarled.

The driver stopped his loading and asked, "Doesn't he cooperate otherwise?"

"Yeah, yeah, yeah. He sees to it that things are taken care of, but all we need is some bureaucrat investigating the accident!" Oblensky stated.

The driver stepped back. "It was an accident, wasn't it?" his voice changing to a note of anxiety.

"Hell, yes! It was an accident," Oblensky shouted.

The driver stared at him and asked, "So what's the concern about an investigation?" as he slammed down the lid of the trunk.

Oblensky dodged around the side of the car, opening the door, ducking inside, and shutting the door with a loud bang. The driver stood staring at the spot that Oblensky had occupied. He shook his head as if to clear his thinking, then opened the driver's door and stepped in. The engine started and the car moved out into the traffic lane.

Before Lee could look around, Brad was there, getting into the back seat, his bag at his side.

"The license plate is BLO612," he said.

"Right," Lee agreed. He, too, had made note of it.

Traffic was heavy. Bob, who was usually a cautious driver, abandoned his cautious ways to keep a visual distance from the car they followed. They came to and went past Seattle, almost. Taking the Elliot Avenue exit, they skirted the north side of the city to the waterfront, followed it along, then turned off to Fisherman's Terminal, stopping at the West Wall, where a large trawler was moored.

"What now?" Bob asked.

"Drive past. We can get the name of the vessel, and if the fellow owns his car, we can get his name as well from the license plate number. That's a start," Lee said.

"I'll see what I can find out. Maybe find someone who knows the guy," Brad added.

Bob turned the car around. "Well, now that the race is won, we'd better get back to the airport for your car, Brad."

"Heck, don't worry about that. I'll get it; no problem." Brad waved his hand, dismissing it. "This has been a great stroke of luck. We may be able to discover whether the suggested intrigue is all so much bunk or if there's a story here."

"Well, there's something that isn't evident yet," Lee said. "We just heard a tirade by Oblensky about the observer and concern about an investigation."

"Then it wasn't an accident?" Brad blurted out.

"No," Lee hastened to reply. "Oblensky assured the other man that that was an accident, but wouldn't reveal his concern about an investigation."

The next day in Anchorage, Elmer was listening intently on the telephone. "Interesting, interesting," he said. "You say the fellow in the elevator is also Russian? Is he a citizen or working under a green card?"

"He's a citizen, all right. Actually, he seems to be okay; on the up and up; you know. It appears he's involved in an employment deal. Getting jobs for his countrymen. Or perhaps it's the other way around.

Getting workers for the ships. Rumors are rampant that they don't get paid too well in some cases," Lee replied.

"What does he get paid?"

"I couldn't discover that, what, or by whom," Lee answered.

"Where does Oblensky fit into this?" Elmer wondered.

"I couldn't find that information, either," Lee said. "They have to be connected, but I've found no evidence to even suggest it. Everyone seems to know Letkof—that's his name—but not many knew Oblensky, and none could see any connection to the observer program with either."

"Well," Elmer said, "there are a few bits of information. At least a starting point. We do need to find out about Oblensky, and there's no question the two men are involved in a common goal. When you have something substantive, something that might lead to a conclusion, let me know." The tone of his voice was that of a busy man.

"Yes, indeed," Lee agreed, and hung up.

While that was going on in Seattle, Clem Tillion and Jim Branson, still at the hotel, were finishing details of the meeting. They were sitting in the lounge. Clem was scanning the paper for the press report of the council meeting. The reporter was definitely influenced by the opposition to the ITQ proposal in halibut and sable fish that he, Clem, had presented to the council—a proposal submitted to the council by Mark Lundston, of the Seattle long line fleet, to gather the data necessary under the federal act to implement an ITQ program, a system that the Pierce Commission in Canada had arrived at as the only way to control the burgeoning fishery. A press man rushed forward to interview Clem.

"Isn't it true," the interviewer asked, "that you're giving away a resource that belongs to all of the people?"

"No more than giving away the land with the Homestead Act," Clem had replied. "Remember how the cattlemen fought the homesteader, yet those free ranging herds had devastated the land?"

"And isn't it true it will make a few fishermen rich? That it is designed for an elite group?"

"If you think five thousand fishermen is an elite group. There are rich fishermen now. Eighty percent of the fish are caught by twenty percent of the fishermen. That's a hard, cold fact of competence. Rules would not change that. I care about the resource. I want there to be a fishery for my great-grandchildren's great-grandchildren. Gordon Jensen has always voted on the side of the fish, too, and he's a fisherman, but he's also concerned for his industry's future."

109

"Aren't you setting up a system that will allow big companies to take over, squeezing the little guy out?" the man persisted.

"No. The quota will be divided for vessel size and will not be transferable from one size to another. In other words, the smallest size can only sell to another fisherman in that category, the next size up to their category, and so on. There is built-in protection for the small vessel. I wouldn't consider not protecting our local fishing fleet."

But the reports in the newspaper echoed the reporter's bias, not the information as presented.

Clem set the paper aside. He sighed. "The logic is always based on the fear that someone might get rich or the premise that they don't want things to change. It's so tiresome. There is no 'then' and 'now.' Times change constantly. Management is our only hope. I recall that in 1904, Dr. David Jordon called attention to the appalling condition of the fishery and the inadequacy of existing conservation measures. He was saying the same thing then that we are saying now. We faced the same argument for limited entry in salmon, and yet that fishery has reached record returns. I know that Governor Hammond, a House member then, faced the same thing when he submitted the Anadromous Fish Act to the early State Legislature. They were still talking about it when I went in, yet it is the backbone of the function of the Department of Fish and Game even today."

"Come on, Tillion; it's an old song to you. Eighteen years in the Legislature has to have taught you something."

"Right. Have another martini."

"Speaking of making money," Branson said, "here comes Bob Thorstenson. Someone from Kodiak was asking me about Icicle Seafoods the other day. I guess I have a rough idea of their history, but I'd rather get it from the boss," he said, waving Bob to the table.

"It's pretty simple," Bob said, settling down into a chair. "Of course, it wasn't always easy—basically because of the timing; and yet if times hadn't been tough, we would never have made it. In 1965, timing made it possible. When we set up the cannery in Seward, there was a bit of opposition. I never did understand it, especially after the way Petersburg stood behind us. We named the cannery Seward Fish."

"But Petersburg is a fishing town," Clem said. "Seward is, first of all, a railroad town and their fishing is mostly sport. There is always a segment of society who don't want change."

"True, true," Bob agreed. "In any case, that was in 1970, just five years after we started. Two years later, in 1972, we merged with Petersburg Cold Storage. That really pulled everything together in Petersburg. In 1976, Petersburg Fisheries acquired Sitka Sound Fisheries. That is when we changed to Icicle Seafoods. We were on a roll and bought Alaskan Seafoods at Homer, and changed it to Icicle."

All this transpired while Branson was jotting down the bare facts.

"Is this an interview?" Bob asked, peering at the notepad.

"No; I'd just like the basic information," Branson said, turning the tablet so Bob could see what he had written.

Petersburg Fisheries 1965
Seward Fisheries 1970
Sitka Sound Seafoods 1976 (changed to Icicle)
Alaskan Seafoods 1977

"Well," Branson exclaimed, "you all were both busy and bold."

"We had so much support from our stockholders, our cannery workers, and our fishermen, we could stand behind the market demand," Bob said with pride.

"But you didn't mention any floating processors. That's what my friend was talking about," Branson said, tapping his list with his pen.

"Oh, yes," Bob replied, "we call it the Star Division."

Branson quickly wrote: "Star Division."

"That was in 1979," Bob said.

Branson added 1979 and Bob continued, "We felt it was the way to go to keep up with the fishery constantly moving westward. Some felt it was a mistake with the rising interest rates. I don't agree." The expression of adamant determination crossed Bob's countenance. "We just have to hang in there. I'm sure there's a way through this, just like there was in the beginning. The fishery is so rich in the North Pacific that a processor simply can't go wrong to be there," he said with conviction.

"Do you agree with all this talk about quotas and limits?" Jim asked.

"I believe that only the management that sustains the resource should be considered. Fishermen will fish however the system is if there are fish to catch," Bob replied.

"Did anyone ever suggest you were bullheaded?" Branson asked.

Bob laughed. "What makes you ask that?" he asked, and they all laughed.

"Some people say Icicle is grabby and piggy, gobbling up all of the opportunities," Branson said.

Bob stared at him for a long moment. "Then they only see its success in terms of dollars. They haven't given any thought to what Petersburg Fisheries means to Alaskan communities and to the fishermen. We set out to sustain and build an economy for Petersburg, and then for Alaska and Alaskans. We've done that with hard work and faith in what we're doing. I can't get upset if someone is jealous. We've all worked hard and are still working. Have we made money? Of course, and we will, hopefully, continue to do so. Opportunities are always there if one is willing to take the risk and do the work. Right now I'm sweating out the interest rates. I can't sit back and relax. I don't want to. It's my life."

There was nothing either man could say in reply to this solid statement of fact. There was no loophole for "what of," "maybe," or even "why."

"They say you are lucky," Clem said, laughing, knowing how ridiculous that was in the face of Bob's relentless efforts.

Bob didn't reply at first, except to make a sweeping gesture of dismissal. Then he leaned forward and said, "Perhaps that's true. I had Pam and a town like Petersburg behind me."

"That's what America is founded on," Clem stated. "Brains, hard work, and guts."

A year later, in 1982, Jim Branson was standing in the dressing room of a Japanese hot spring bathhouse. He hung his coat on a hook provided for that and started to unbutton his shirt. "I don't know, Tillion, what you're getting us into," Jim said, as he peered around the brilliantly white, super-clean dressing room with its rows of lockers along one wall for the clothes they were removing. At this moment, Jim Branson, Lee Alverson, Gordon Jensen, Bob Thorstenson, and Clem Tillion were the only men in the room. Gordon towered over them all, his six-foot-seven frame not fat, but massive. The others' average height hovered around six feet.

Clem ignored Jim's remark. He was happy to be back again to the pleasure of the hot springs. Lee, Jim, and Clem had flown to the northern island of Hokkaido that day for a pleasure trip before they had to return to Tokyo, where the International North Pacific Fisheries Commission would hold its annual meeting. The day before, Bob Thorstenson and Gordon had come separately. They had all been toured across the island to see the cranes—huge beautiful, black-and-white birds, with their brilliant red top knot, that were feeding in a farmer's stubble field. Then they toured Hokkaido to visit fish plants and lumber yards. The trip to the hot springs was icing on the cake. Clem quickly draped a huge white towel around his middle as he removed the last of

112

his clothes, placing them in a locker. He headed for the door to the bathhouse. "See you inside," he stated cheerfully.

The other four were right behind him. They all stood for a moment adjusting their sight to the steamy room. It was like a huge cave. The steam obliterated the ceiling and, for the most part, the walls. Clem crossed the tiled floor to a long trough of water inset into it. There were small dipping buckets and low stools around the perimeter. He threw his towel aside, sat down, filled a bucket with water and poured it over his shoulders. He picked up a bar of soap from a dish and lathered himself, filling another bucket with water and rinsing off. "This is so you are clean when you get into the pool," Clem explained. "We'll shower, too," he said, nodding toward the jets of water spraying from a multitude of holes in a long pipe.

When they were all finished washing and had stood under the shower, which was more forceful and hotter than they'd expected, they were properly warmed to step into one of the several pools available. "They are each a different temperature. I think we'd best take the middle ground here," Clem advised, throwing his towel over the low cement rail that ran adjacent to the pools.

There were other men in the pools, Japanese, for the most part, in the hotter section.

"Yeow!" Bob gasped as he stepped in. "Good grief; what would the first pool be like?"

"Ever been in a Finnish sauna?" Gordon asked.

As they sank into the water, they heard a comment from one of the Japanese in English, whispered loudly. "Look out! Tsunami!" Even they laughed.

They sank into the water to their necks, almost floating with spontaneous sighs of pleasure and relaxation. They sank down over their heads, coming up like surfacing seals, brushing the strands of wet hair out of their eyes. They grinned at each other, wet hair plastered to their foreheads, cheeks shiny wet, smiles that said they felt a little foolish, but wasn't it fun?

"Lordy," Lee sighed, "this reminds me of my childhood in Hawaii."

"You're from Hawaii?" Jim asked, surprised.

"We lived there when I was a kid. My father had a radio station at Hilo. There were few haoles. [That's what they call white folk.] My brother and I had our own canoe. We could buy hook, line, and bait for five cents. We were as Hawaiian as the rest of the boys. When the tour ships came in, we would pick fruit and paddle out to sell to the tourists." Lee's face held a dreamy expression in recall.

"I guess you go back there often," Jim commented.

Lee laughed. "Actually, I didn't go back for thirty years. I went into the Navy in February of 1942. I felt so grown up, and looked like a kid!

"Spent two years behind the lines in China. We helped a lot of people. It was heartbreaking and exciting at the same time. I went back to China fifty years later. Actually got to step onto the island we were trying to take. Maybe the only man from our ship, the *Sockeye Six,* to make it. Anyway, I came back and went to school at San Diego, then to the University of Washington School of Fisheries. I had some romantic notion a job in fisheries would be out-of-doors, so it was thirty years before I took Ruby over to see Hilo. One of my old buddies knew me right off and yelled, 'Hiya, Lee; how's your brother?'"

Bob Thorstenson pushed the wet hair back off his forehead. "That reminds me of rowing out to the fishing boats off Point Roberts when I was ten. I traded fresh vegetables and fruit for fish."

"So you really were a farm boy," Lee observed.

"Well, half and half. My grandfather fished cod off the coast of Iceland. He was the foreman of an open boat off the coast of Vik. When he came to Point Roberts, he intended to fish and farm. He and his partner built a gillnet boat and they began fishing. However, about that

time, traps were perfected and canneries didn't buy fish from fishermen, so they had to work in the canneries and sell produce. My father, Laugi, worked for Alaska Packers as a teenager. He was a tender skipper at the age of twenty. His generation almost entirely went to sea. After the heyday in Puget Sound and after traps were eliminated in 1934, he went to Alaska. The traps were already gone when I was rowing out to the fishing boats."

"I guess we all experienced the sea when we were kids," Gordon observed. "Me in Alaska, Lee in Hawaii, Clem in New York, Bob at Point Roberts, and Jim in Oregon."

"And could be why we're all here at this moment," Clem said. "And speaking of why we are here, I noticed that the joint venture bycatch figures had doubled since last year's report."

"At least by what has been reported," Gordon stated bluntly.

"I think those observers are very conscientious," Lee protested.

"Maybe," Gordon said, "but rumors get around. Don't forget; H. Heward Bell says halibut stocks are really threatened by the bottom trawls. What do you think?"

Lee scowled. "Come on, Gordon. You know it's an anxious scene. The potential for overcapitalization in the fleet is like a freight train coming down the track. We've already seen it on the East Coast. I suppose what you're really asking me is why hasn't the scientific community advocated outlawing bottom trawls."

Gordon pursed his lips and raised his eyebrows in a questioning expression.

"Well, my friend," Lee said, "too often we, in the scientific community, are wrapped up in exact data. Is there proof positive that the bottom trawls caused the decline? Only the political arena can make arbitrary decisions."

"Right," Gordon said. "Funny, isn't it? We expect them to tell us what to do, and they wait for the data to tell them. And then it's too late."

"Now, now," Lee protested, "fishermen will fish until the last fish is caught. The sad thing is that the guy who goes to bat for the conservative side—perhaps even to err on the side of conservation, and not just talk about it—is always met with howls of opposition. The strongest voice always is money. The fisherman's living, the scientists' funding, and the industry's profit margin. It's the same old story from the beginning of time. It was so easy to address when INPFC first started and we didn't have to fight our own people, just the foreign fleet."

Gordon heaved a big sigh and sank down into the water as if to wash away the anxieties attached to fisheries management.

116

Fifteen minutes later, Jim, looking at his waterproof watch, warned, "We'd better hustle along here; our flight to Tokyo won't wait for us."

They quickly dried and dressed. Much refreshed, they hustled to the car that waited for them. At Chitose Airport, they were shocked to see, looming above the crowd, the heads of Oblensky and Letkof.

Oblensky was leaning toward Letkof, shaking his finger to emphasize whatever he was saying, his face flushed with the urgency of it. Letkof stared intently at him, nodding occasionally. They moved off to the gate for their flight.

"What the heck are they doing here?" Clem gasped. "I hope he isn't going to be at the meetings."

After they had gotten their seat assignments and also moved toward the gate for their flight to Tokyo, they saw that the two men were waiting at the same gate. How could they remain unnoticed?

"Well, unless we lie down on the floor, we're visible," Bob pointed out.

"I'm going to find out what they are doing here," Clem said, leaving before anyone could reply.

"I say there, Oblensky," Clem hailed the man, "what brings you to Japan?"

Oblensky was taken by surprise, a position he was not at all comfortable with. He looked around. There was no way he could escape the greeter. "Just traveling through," Oblensky mumbled, then turned away to speak to Letkof.

"Mr. Letkof," Clem persisted, "what are you doing in Japan?"

Letkof looked desperately at Oblensky as if for guidance. Oblensky grabbed him by the shoulder and turned him away from Clem, too. Letkof jerked away from Oblensky's hand, mumbling something sharply. He spun around and, looking at Clem, said, "Actually, we are returning from the Far East. My family members are there. And you?"

Clem smiled. "We're here for meetings," indicating the others.

"Oh, yes, the Old Boys Club," Oblensky growled when he saw them, quite a distance away, talking to each other. "Reminiscing, no doubt."

"I expect you were delighted to see the reports from the joint ventures," Clem said in a genial voice.

The two men looked at each other, startled.

"Well, yes, we were," Letkof said.

"It looks like it's going to keep you busy finding enough men for those ships, and taking care of that bycatch," Clem added. "Well, I'd

117

better get back. Don't want to miss any good stories," he said, his guess verified.

Oblensky turned on Letkof. "Did you tell him what we're doing?" he asked, his face red and his voice angry.

"No. I never saw the guy before," Letkof protested. "What difference does it make?"

"The difference it makes, you dumbbell, is that they're after us," Oblensky snarled. "If you never saw him before, how did he know your name?"

Letkof looked startled. "You're right. How did he know? You take care of the details for the workers, so what business is it of theirs?" His expression changed to one of concern. "You do take care of the details?" he asked. "What did he mean about bycatch?"

"It's that female thing, the observer thing," Oblensky growled, ignoring Letkof's question. "They just don't understand." He scowled at Letkof. "Haven't we done well? Haven't you done well working for me?"

"Yes, yes," Letkof replied, all too familiar with Oblensky's temper.

The line was forming to board the flight. They moved across the

room to join it. Oblensky glanced around to see where the big Americans were. "Bastards," he mumbled. "Self-satisfied bastards."

At the Tokyo airport, Lee, Bob, Clem, Jim, and Gordon quickly made their way to the monorail that swiftly traverses the distance between the airport and the city; elevated to be free of the massive volume of traffic on the streets below. At their station, they hailed two cabs, flashing their hotel cards to indicate the destination.

At the hotel, they agreed to meet for dinner and went to their separate rooms.

Later, back in the lobby of the New Imperial Hotel, they found Elmer Rasmuson and Harold Lokken in the company of two very important Japanese businessmen who were always present at the fisheries meetings.

"Well, hello there," Bob said, surprised to see the two men, knowing they were no longer on the commission. "Don't think we can manage it without you?" he laughed, then sobered. "You may be right."

Elmer chuckled. "We had some other business and thought we'd also have the pleasure of your company," Elmer said, making a gesture that included them all. "These gentlemen have requested we all dine together," he said. "They have suggested an excellent restaurant. Would you care to join us?"

They looked at each other and smiled their agreement, bowing slightly to the two Japanese, who returned the gesture, smiling their pleasure.

The dinner provided the finest of Japanese cuisine. Although it was not the usual ceremonial affair with hostesses for each man, the dishes were beautifully presented.

The conversation was cheerful, and with the excuse of a bit of saki, one of the Japanese expressed a delightful sense of humor rather than the usual watchful austerity. Between laughter and one-liners, he would make an observation, a statement that could be acknowledged with an answer, or ignored, always giving the others at the table a choice.

At one point, the Japanese gentleman lifted his glass and announced, "Mr. Lokken has been with us for many years. A toast," while extending his glass to Harold.

"Here, here," they all cheered, and Harold suppressed his sense of pleasure by looking down at his own glass but flushing ever so slightly.

"A rare commodity," Elmer said, raising his glass again. "To a modest man." Even Harold laughed, in spite of himself.

Back at the hotel, reluctant to say good night, they settled down in the posh lounge chairs of the lobby.

"INPFC isn't enough now. We can't complain about the fact that it curbed the foreign fleet and that the Magnuson Act provided additional ability to administer better management, but it is a never-ending battle. If we could just guess what the fishing effort would be ten years down the road and start the regulatory process with foresight instead of hindsight," Clem stated.

"Regulations must be based on factual data," Lee pointed out. "If we did arbitrarily impose regulations without proof of the need, it could go both ways. Regulators change. Technology has been the biggest factor. It changes so rapidly to provide access to the sea from the bottom up. It isn't a guessing game anymore."

"Right," Clem agreed. "Remember how our Japanese friends told us, when Elmer and Negraponte negotiated the move to 175 E for salmon, that we'd better be prepared to can a lot of salmon. We expected an increase perhaps from four million to twelve. They came in at fifty-six million red salmon. That fishery has been sustained, although I think the intercept fishery now, with that new technology, is going to have devastating effects on Bristol Bay."

"That is a social problem. Who gets the fish?" Jim pointed out.

"I know," Clem acknowledged, "but it also is a potential problem for the river system's escapement. There are a lot of major rivers, as well as the Yukon. I make no bones about feeling protective of Alaskans, those are our fish, but no one gains if they are stopped before they even come near their home stream. The Japanese intercept shows that."

"I'm just as worried about those bottom trawls—the damage they do and the bycatch that is destroyed must have an accumulative effect," Gordon said firmly. "Some guys say they can't harvest certain species any other way. Well, I guess I think if they can figure out how to go to the moon, someone can figure that out."

"It's so strange," Harold said in a thoughtful voice. "We have the richest waters in the world and our fishery has a deficit, according to the National Advisory Committee on Oceans and Atmosphere report, of 2.9 billion dollars in 1981. It doesn't seem to add up. I'm never sure just what costs are involved in those figures. But having served on NACOA, I believe their report. They have no ax to grind."

"I think we should turn fisheries management over to Bob, here. He seems to be able to set a goal and stick to it," Lee said with a chuckle. They all smiled and nodded. "The big issue now is quality control. We can't compete with the products of Norway, Japan, and other nations who have very sophisticated processing methods."

"And some that are very simple, like how the fisherman handles the fish he catches," Clem said. "When we were in Denmark, we visited the Faroes and saw that the fishermen there never stacked one fish on top of another. They were bled and placed in a tote side by side; then another tote was stacked on top with another single layer of fish. That is how they were delivered by the fisherman. Hardly a comparison to our set netters that throw the fish into a truck or the gill netters that toss them into the hold of the boat and then pitch them out again. It certainly made our system seem prehistoric. It comes down to the fact that we have never considered the consumer."

Elmer nodded. "Times change."

"By the way, we saw that man Oblensky in Chitose Airport," Lee said.

Elmer turned to him with a quick look of interest. "Did you find out about him?"

Jim leaned forward. "Yes. We did learn that when he left Petersburg, he tried Juneau. Had a kid with him, a boy. No one seemed to know about the wife. He then went into the Interior up near Bethel. He must have made contacts because he got a government job, some sort of socioeconomic thing. The boy went to law school and now lives in Juneau. He's apparently doing well. Has a family. He's the father of the steward on the ship."

"What about Oblensky now?" Elmer interrupted.

"Well, we just learned that he seems to have a business of slipping foreigners, particularly Russians or Poles, into the high seas fleet as workers on trawlers and factory ships," Jim said. "And he's possibly involved with the sale of bycatch over the side."

"And the fellow that was with him is the man I saw in the elevator. He's apparently his partner or works for him, or at least was with him," Lee volunteered.

"He said he had been visiting his family in Russia," Clem added.

Elmer looked thoughtful. "Hmmm," he murmured. "That all sounds quite plausible, but not a clue about the involvement of the observer—unless that's connected to the sale of bycatch over the side. He may have found that women aren't as easily persuaded to look the other way. Oh well, as Lee says, it all seems too theatrical." Elmer leaned forward. "I think I shall retire." He stood up to leave and they all followed suit, bidding each other good night.

As Elmer walked down the corridor of the New Imperial Hotel, he thought of the Old Imperial Hotel, designed by Frank Lloyd Wright prior to the devastating earthquake in 1924 that leveled most of Tokyo. To withstand earthquakes, it was designed with interlocking corners that allowed the building to flex. He, Elmer, had the privilege of staying in that hotel before it was torn down to accommodate the sky-scraper hotel needed now for the traveling population. The entrance to that old hotel still remained, but photographers and artists were seen every day recording its elegance before it, too, was discarded to accommodate the needs of change.

As Elmer approached a corner of the corridor, he heard a gruff, angry voice and a placating but insistent response from around the bend. He stopped, not wanting to intrude. He looked back down the length of the hall he'd traversed, but felt too tired to retrace his steps. He sighed wearily and leaned against the wall to wait for a convenient time to continue on to his room. His attention was caught by the word "female" spoken with disgust and contempt. He moved closer to the corner to listen.

"They're so damned picky. You tell them something. Mind you, they're working for you. You're not working for them. You tell them to add ex-pounds of some kind of fish to the order, and they say they won't, or it's too much, or it's not *right*. For God's sake, what *is* right, I ask you? And then the bitch tells you she has to tally everything. What

can you do with a person like that? People are hungry; they need fish. It's going to waste, anyway, so what's the gripe? She . . ." he sputtered.

His companion took advantage of the pause. "Look, Viktor, she's dead. There'll be a new observer, and you can either work something out or cancel that ship. That isn't the only one of our available sources."

"But," Oblensky growled, "if it's another female, I refuse to deal with her. They're so stupid. I could just wring their scrawny necks."

"Now, Viktor, that's a poor attitude. We have to work with the system. We have to appear in compliance at all times."

"My word," Elmer thought, "that's Oblensky!"

"But I fear they'll send another one of those damned females who can't keep her mouth shut and just do her job," Viktor growled. "I begged the council to not allow women. The accident was proof enough of their inadequacy. But they wouldn't listen. Bunch of damn dumbbells."

"Surely your grandson can help. I assume you got him that job for that purpose," Viktor's companion said.

"My grandson," Viktor choked, "my grandson is a wishy-washy bookworm. He spends all his time studying the damn business instead of doing it. He's as useless as that lousy girl was. No. My grandson is worthless. He admired that girl for working on the ship. He doesn't get it."

"Well, Viktor, no sense beating your head against the wall. Let me know what the story will be about the ship's tally. The incidental figures look good and the price is right. I'm tired. Tomorrow is a busy day. I'm going to bed," Viktor's companion said.

Elmer turned around so his back would be to the approaching figure if he came around the corner. Soon he heard a door open and quickly spun around to get a glimpse as it closed; taking note of the number.

Elmer retraced his steps down the hall. He was elated. There it was. He's selling fish as well as labor. Poor grandson, having a grandfather like that. Must have some good blood in there somewhere, though. But why was the girl working for him? Why did he say that?

A door he had just passed opened. He spun around when he heard the knob click. One of the scientific group of INPFC stepped out.

"Well, hi there, Elmer. You headed for the sack?"

"Yes, indeed. It's been a long day."

Inside his room, Elmer closed the door, checked the lock, and leaned against it. He sighed, then smiled. "I dare say that isn't the first dialogue of international intrigue to take place in this hotel."

Six

Elmer Rasmuson was a man of action. "I must find out who the other man is," he mumbled as he brushed his teeth, after showering and preparing for bed. "Gordon has been flagging this bycatch for years. Since that fellow is staying here, perhaps I will see him at breakfast. Perhaps I can find out at the desk," he determined.

Breakfast was in the hotel coffee shop, which was a busy place—people hurrying to eat to go to work; people meeting others to talk business or pleasure, besides the usual parade of tourist customers.

Elmer was soon joined by members of the fisheries group—from INPFC, not those cognizant of Oblensky, so he said nothing of the evening's revelation. He constantly scanned the room, listening intently to catch the cadence of that voice he'd heard the night before.

"You worried about our progress, Elmer?" one of the men asked. "You seem edgy."

"No, no," Elmer replied. "Sorry. I was looking for someone I thought might be here this morning. Obviously he is not." He sighed and turned his attention to the ongoing discussion about fisheries.

When Elmer left the dining room, he went to the front desk. Giving his name and room number, he asked if he might inquire who had the room nearby, giving the clerk the number. He was sure he'd heard a familiar voice, but couldn't remember the name.

The Japanese desk clerk's expression was blank as he replied, "I'm sorry; we can't divulge the names of our guests. Perhaps he will have heard your voice." A flicker of humor crossed his countenance.

Elmer smiled and nodded his thanks. *Oh well; it was a try,* he thought, and went to his room to prepare for the meeting. There was a message from Dr. Lee Alverson. "Need to talk," it said.

Elmer had been reluctant to call anyone to talk about his new discovery over the phone. This was fortuitous. He called Lee's room. No one was there. He hurried down to join the group gathering for the meeting.

"Received your message," Elmer said to Lee. "Let's have lunch. Perhaps in my room we can talk."

Later, when the two men turned the corner of the corridor leading to Elmer's room, they saw a bellboy stacking luggage on a cart from the room across the hall from Elmer's room. The door was open. They could hear a man's voice, obviously on the telephone, by the commanding sound of it. "Yes, yes. I'm leaving, but I'll meet you for lunch at the Sanno. No, I . . ." Elmer pulled Lee back around the corner. "That's him. We have to get to the Sanno as quickly as we can. Come on!" he said, striding back down the way they had come.

Lee hurried after him. "Who?" he asked. "Who is 'he?'"

"You'll find out," Elmer stated. He rushed to the hotel entrance and hailed a cab. The cab's door flew open and the two men stepped in.

"To the Sanno," Elmer ordered. "Quickly," he added.

The cab driver sped up, weaving in and out of the traffic. "Is this necessary?" Lee asked, overwhelmed by the taxi driver's skill and daring. "There's a belief that all those Japanese kamikaze pilots who survived the war are now the taxi drivers."

Elmer ignored the joke. "If we can get there and be situated in an inconspicuous location, we have a chance to burst Oblensky's balloon. I'll tell you about it when we get there."

The Sanno was the U.S. military officer's billet in Tokyo, and was available to the few fisheries men who were State Department advisors with GS18 rating. When they arrived at the drive, Elmer flashed his card and they were waved in. He paid the cab driver and they hurried into the lobby to find seats at a good location to see the lobby door but not be conspicuous. There were other men here and there watching television or reading.

Elmer didn't know what the man would look like. He only knew the sound of his voice. He hoped the other man would be Oblensky.

"Hey," Lee said. "Look over there. It's that lawyer from Juneau. How did he get in here?"

"We can't get into a conversation now. We have to remain as quiet as a mouse. You'll get your chance. He doesn't look like he's leaving," Elmer said, nodding toward the Juneau man.

"What is going on?" Lee asked.

Elmer was looking at everyone, wondering if each one might be the man. "You see," Elmer explained, "last night when I went to my room, I overheard Oblensky complaining bitterly to the man we heard in the room near mine. I was coming down the hall and stopped when I heard them. I thought they were arguing and did not want to intrude. Then I realized that the loudmouth was Oblensky. He was complaining about the girl, and the other voice was talking about getting product—obviously, the 'incidental catch.' If we can see who he is, we can track down that illegal operation. By the way, what was it you had on your mind?"

Lee scoffed, "Nothing compared to this event."

Elmer held out his hand. "Here comes a taxi."

They watched the cab driver unload luggage from the trunk of the car. A bellboy rushed out with a cart. The man paid the taxi driver and turned to come into the lobby.

The man was a lawyer from Washington, D.C., well-known to both Elmer and Lee. Elmer and Lee gasped. They simultaneously turned away from the direction of the door and held their heads down as if to examine something.

"My word. Now what?" Lee gasped. "Are you sure that's the one? You said you didn't recognize his voice," he said, not wanting to believe it.

"It's the one. Look at the luggage. I'm sure his voice is not one I have reason to recall." They watched the man enter the dining room to join the man from Juneau.

They sat back and stared at each other. "Well, well, well," Elmer said. "I don't exactly feel like slinking away. Let's go see what they have to say."

"Why not?" Lee stated.

They walked briskly into the dining room. A waitress stepped forward to escort them to a table. As they passed nearby, the D.C. lawyer spoke up. "I say there, Elmer. How nice to see you here. In fact," he said, looking at Lee, "to see two of my most favorite people. Care to join us?" he asked, gesturing toward the two empty chairs at their table.

Elmer took the extended hand and nodded to the other man. "Thank you, no. Dr. Alverson and I have things to discuss. What brings you to Japan?" he asked.

"Routine business. I'm showing Joe, here, the ropes. He's doing some work for us. You know how it is. Every country has its own way of doing business."

"Oh," Elmer said, looking at Joe. "Oil or fish?" he asked.

"We don't even know, ourselves, yet," the D.C. lawyer butted in quickly, with bland good humor. "This is a systems training session. You know how it is," he repeated.

"Ah, yes. Yes, I do," Elmer replied. "I'm surprised that you haven't attended the INPFC meetings. Bring yourself up to date on management. Joint ventures are the big thing now. I understand that some agreements have been made so all the bycatch doesn't go to waste."

The lawyer's face froze into a polite, blank expression. "I've heard that there have been some international negotiations about that," he said.

Elmer nodded his head, pursing his lips in a thoughtful expression. "Yes, it seemed to me that someone said you were involved. But you know how it is; I dare say it's easy to get one lawyer mixed with another."

"I dare say," the lawyer murmured, then picked up the menu.

Elmer started to walk away, then turned back to the table. "Oh, yes; now I remember. It was that fellow, Oblensky. Seemed like he was in charge of the observer end of the negotiations."

The lawyer looked at Elmer with disgust. "That, of course, is ridiculous. He can barely tie his shoes."

"Oh, you know him then," Elmer observed.

"Who doesn't?" the lawyer said, forcing a smile.

"I admit I was surprised. I couldn't imagine that he would be involved in something so important. He must have been bragging to impress someone. Nice to see you again," Elmer said. "Pay attention, young man," he said to Joe. "Your instructor, here, is a pro." Elmer then moved along to their designated table where Lee was already seated.

Three meeting days later, sitting in the Tokyo airport, an hour prior to departure, Clem, Jim, and Gordon watched Bob Thorstenson moving about, talking first to one and then to another of the delegation or members of the industry.

Elmer and Lee stood waiting for an opportunity to squeeze in beside them in the crowded terminal. "Did you tell them?" Elmer asked.

"No. I'll hold on this until there is some circumspect way to check it through. Shades of the old salmon trap days. Washington holds the key. History repeats itself once again," Lee said.

"I wish they were all like Thorstenson over there," Elmer stated, nodding toward Bob. "He's done very well for Icicle, operating on the fair and square. He's busy as a bird dog. Everyone else is exhausted," Elmer chuckled.

From across the room, Gordon sighed, "It makes me tired just watching him."

Jim nodded. "Ralph Horde told me some great stories about Bob. Ralph said when he was a new plant manager at Seward, he was always amazed at how much Bob always knew about what was going on around the plant, in the city, and at the fishing grounds, when he'd just arrived after being elsewhere for two to four weeks. He said that he [Ralph] would arrive at the plant every morning at six or six-fifteen and Bob would be there waiting, quizzing him about everything, but he seemed to already know all the answers. It really baffled him until one of the tender skippers told him that Bob would get in late and get up early, like four-thirty, to have breakfast on whatever tender was at the dock, and he'd get all the gossip from the cook, then check it out on Ralph."

They chuckled a little, still watching Bob's progress.

"Right," Gordon said. "Tommy Thompson tells how, when he and Bob were partners, they were traveling about checking on the plants and the fishing grounds, and in general had a very busy day. At the end of the day he was exhausted, but Bob kept pacing back and forth with telephone in hand, looking worried. Tommy asked him what was wrong; it seemed to him everything was going perfectly. Bob replied, 'I know; the problem is, who should I call now?' That's Bob! Never passes up anyone he thinks he should talk to."

Bob's head spun around to look at them, as if sensing their conversation about him. They smiled and nodded, and he turned back to the three Japanese men he was talking to.

"Well, he'll have to hurry to finish this crowd!" Clem laughed, looking at the hundreds of people milling about the terminal.

Home again, in Seattle, Lee Alverson rushed down to his office. It

128

had been two years, almost, since he'd become independent; establishing the Natural Resource Consultant, Inc., business after a lifetime of academic fisheries research, teaching—in the United States as well as in many foreign countries—plus federal fisheries management. But it was still exciting to drive into the parking lot and see the sign indicating his business among the others housed in the building, including the *National Fisherman's Magazine* office.

"Hello there," Brad greeted Lee, as he walked past. "How was Japan?"

"It was pretty much a hold on what we've already accomplished. Lots of talk about joint ventures," Lee said. He looked around when he heard the door of his office open. His secretary stepped out.

"Lee, I'm so glad you're back. Your desk is a mountain of paper, and some fellow will be here at four-thirty to see you; he had a Polish name, sounded interesting. Sorry to interrupt," the secretary said and shut the door.

"Looks like I'd better get to work," Lee said.

"Let's have a chat about joint ventures sometime soon," Brad suggested.

"Sure," Lee agreed. "Let me get that mountain of paper sorted out." He looked at his watch. "How about a coffee break in two hours?"

"Right on," Brad agreed. "We can have it right here," he said, waving his arm at the space of his office. He was eager to tell Brad what had happened in Tokyo, but knew that Elmer would handle the situation best—and the less said, the better.

Lee was ready for a coffee break after two hours of studying proposals, data sheets, time schedules, and correspondence in general. He shuffled the papers into two tidy piles and walked briskly along the veranda to Brad's office. "We saw that fellow Oblensky in Japan," Lee said as he opened the door.

"So," Brad asked, ignoring Lee's train of thought, "what's the scoop on joint ventures? Lots of rumors flying around about slipping product, bycatch product, over the side to foreign buyers, of crews not getting paid their full share, and such."

Lee chuckled, "You've dumped a real load on me there. I'll begin by saying the joint ventures are working very well. The processing ships have their quota. The Japanese were very amazed to see how many U.S. trawlers and processors were getting into the game. As you know, they are out as soon as the U.S. fleet can handle the TAC. They aren't keen on us being such quick learners. I think the cheating, just like it always has been, in any business, is done by cheaters—the salmon creek robbers; the pot fisherman who sets early, using drift logs for

129

buoys and all the other tricks he dreams up. As for fair pay, I don't know what can be done to make companies pay their fair share. That's a personal matter between employer and employee."

"I heard of one vessel that's tied up for not paying the crew a fair share. Last report, they were settling out of court," Brad said.

"Who was that?" Lee asked.

"I don't know. The crew's lawyer told me. Wouldn't divulge that detail. We were talking about the situation," Brad replied. "It's a big ocean out there. They buy at sea and sell at sea. It could be very easy to deliver to a foreign ship without anyone knowing. Of course, the observer would know, I should think. Any crew member who might be interested enough to learn how the system works would, too. Do you think the observers turn their backs?" Brad asked.

Lee looked thoughtful. "Obviously, it would be possible. However, their job is to record catch. They are not enforcement officers. Most ships have two observers."

"Do I pick up a defensive note?" Brad asked with a smile.

"Perhaps," Lee said and smiled back. "However, they are in an academic role. Those types are rarely devious. In fact, we ran into that man, Oblensky, at Sapporo. Found out he's a middleman for hiring crew for the ships—foreigners, that is. He was coming from Russia; had his sidekick with him. Unpleasant man."

"How many joint venture processors are there?" Brad asked.

"This year there are fifty-three," Lee answered, then stood up. "I've got to get back to work. Thanks for the coffee. I'm sure, like always, it will boom very quickly. I have to say, I was proud of American ingenuity, even if the outcome will be overfishing and subsequent restrictions."

"It never seems to fail, but one can always hope. Well, let me know when you find out anything new on Oblensky," Brad said.

Lee had just settled down at his desk when the door flew open.

"Dr. Alverson, I believe." Oblensky, effusively cordial, stepped into Lee's office. "Viktor Oblensky is my name," he said as he extended his hand.

Lee stood up and leaned across the desk to shake Oblensky's hand. "What can I do for you?" Lee asked, his expression reserved.

"Information," Viktor Oblensky said.

"What sort of information?" Lee asked.

"Biological, of course, Dr. Alverson," Oblensky declared, seating himself comfortably as if to spend a good bit of time there. "I know who you are, of course. Everyone does. What a fine scientist.

"Now, I'm small potatoes in this fish business," Oblensky contin-

130

ued, "but my job with the state of Alaska occasionally demands that I know a little bit. I have friends in the joint venture business but that doesn't help with what I need to know. They are fishermen, not scientists." His expression was humble and sincere.

"And what is your job?" Lee asked.

"Economic development," Oblensky replied. "We work with the villages. I'm upriver, you know, on the Kuskokwim, near Bethel."

"What is it you want to know?" Lee asked.

"As you know, the people on the river live by and on fish, in every respect. Well, now, what we need, with these new joint venture things going on, is some biological data that can tell us if they are taking our fish out there before they reach the river. You know, some chart or graph, or something. I mean, if they are hitting our run, we need to protest. Those people only have fish."

Lee stared at the man. If he had not known his business, he might have been moved by his begging expression and plea for the good of the people on the river.

"Of course I could research data that show where the main fish stocks are, but the Alaska Department of Fish and Game has that information, too. Why are you asking for my advice? Your state has everything you need," Lee stated.

Oblensky laughed a small, self-effacing, laugh. "Well, shoot; I was here in Seattle, anyway. I saw you in Japan with the other fellows and just flashed on the fact that you'd have, right at your fingertips, the information I want for my people."

Lee's expression hardened. "There did seem to be some suggestion that you were involved with finding foreign workers for the joint venture ships. What about that?"

Oblensky scoffed, "Oh, that's my friend. I was with him because he invited me to go to Russia with him to visit family. I have Russian relatives, too, even though I'm mostly Polish," making a gesture like sweeping away such a thought.

"I see," Lee replied. He sat back in his chair. "You know, speaking of Japan, I ran across a fellow there who said he works with you. Something to do with the observers being kept up to step on the international scene of selling bycatch. It wasn't all too clear. How does that work?" he asked.

Oblensky stared at Lee. "Well, uh, I uhm, . . . I am sometimes a go-between for the big boys just because I know the industry. I don't enjoy having to deal with those observers, especially the females. You may have heard, one of them just stumbled and killed herself. She was so clumsy." Oblensky pulled himself together, his expression changing back to one of the pleading innocent. "Never mind that. Could you please provide me with that salmon data?" he begged.

Lee leaned forward and, picking up some papers, appeared to be closing the discussion. "No. Actually it would take me a month, with the other work stacked up here, just to get to it. You'd best get it from your own Department of Fish and Game. They will have it right on file."

Oblensky's face turned a deep red color. "You can't refuse me those figures," he almost shouted.

"Well, actually, I can. I'm in private business here," Lee said quietly. "You just check in Juneau. They'll have all the information you need."

Oblensky stared at Lee for a long moment, then stood up to leave. He started to extend his hand and thought the better of it, as Lee had turned to some notes on his desk. Oblensky hurried past the secretary and out the door.

"Whew! Isn't he a charger?" the secretary observed.

Lee stopped by Brad's office as he left, seeing that Brad was still in.

"I thought you'd stop by," Brad said.

"I wanted to before, but you two were at it so intently, I decided to wait. What did he want? He looked like he was close to tears," Brad noted.

"Ah, yes. He was pleading for information on the location of

132

salmon in the Bering Sea to, ah, help his people upriver," Lee explained. "I refused to give it to him. There's just something there. We do know that he does work for the state and that he does live near Bethel, so I couldn't exactly doubt his story. He mentioned seeing me in Japan. He explained that it was his friend who was involved with the joint venture thing, and that he was just on a trip to visit family. Frankly, I think he's covering his tracks."

Brad shook his head. "There was little resemblance today to that bully at the council meeting."

Lee reached for the doorknob. "Well, I'm off to have dinner with Ruby. Taking her to the Space Needle. She likes the view."

"Have fun," Brad said as Lee went out the door.

The next morning, Lee phoned Elmer.

"Elmer, Lee here; what did you learn? Oblensky just stopped by my office to get data on salmon taken as bycatch that might affect his people, the folks on the Kuskokwim and Yukon. I made an excuse not to give it to him. I suspect it's information for his offshore duties. I squeezed it out of him about the bycatch sales and his connection with the observers."

Elmer, taken aback by the outburst, cleared his throat, nodded agreement to Lee's statement, and replied, "Well, Lee, I've had the situation investigated quite thoroughly. It seems there is a history of international exchange of fish for hard currency as well as the food aspect of it prior to the Magnuson Act. And although that has started a dramatic change from the old ways and systems, it won't dissolve overnight. That isn't a statement of approval, but it is a statement of reality and understanding. The fisheries are just beginning to gain a constituency in Washington for conservation as well as harvest via the National Marine Fisheries Service. The lobbyists are still there as they were in the salmon trap days. We witnessed a tiny edge of the big picture. The process is changing, but established systems are slow to vary from what has been an important international pattern."

"You make it sound impossible to do anything about it," Lee said.

"That's right," Elmer replied.

"Well, if it's such an international scene, why would they have a jerk like Oblensky involved?" Lee asked.

"He's undoubtedly very handy for little details—local things, as well as to act as a diversion. He probably doesn't know what the whole picture is. I would guess that he is one of many in that role," Elmer said.

"So much for playing detective. Are you suggesting that management as we wish it is inconsequential?" Lee added.

"Not at all," Elmer said. "Please remember that the changes brought about by the Magnuson Act are not far in the past. I'm sure that the National Marine Fisheries Service is trying to bring about order. The State Department that has handled international affairs is in a far more complex position."

Lee sighed. "As you say, times change. Let's just pray that the cards getting stacked in favor of the resource will be the winning hand."

"Amen," Elmer agreed.

Elmer turned to Mary Louise. "It seems that Oblensky is busy as ever. He wanted salmon data from Lee—information that could be used by the high seas fleet. Lee put him off, although he can simply get it from the Department of Fish and Game. I just can't imagine how he could become involved with any of the observers," Elmer said. "It can't be legal."

"Well, if you really want to find out, you probably could talk to his grandson. If he's as unsympathetic as it sounded like he was, he'd probably tell you," Mary Louise suggested.

Elmer called his friend Jack in Bethel. Did he know the man, or his grandson?

"Strange that you should call right now. The darndest thing happened. Viktor Oblensky just came back from a trip. The Orient, I think. Anyway, his son was here. He's a lawyer, you know; good reputation. They had some sort of a big confrontation, and Viktor literally grabbed his things and stomped out yelling, 'Traitor! Traitor!' according to a couple kids riding by on their bicycles. Scared them. Viktor's son is still here. Looks like he's closing the place down."

"Did he leave Bethel?" Elmer asked.

"Yes. He chartered a plane. Flew to Dillingham to catch a regular flight to Dutch Harbor," Jack said.

"To Dutch Harbor?" Elmer gasped. "What in the world would he be dashing off to Dutch Harbor for ?"

"That's what the agent said. Said he had an important meeting to attend and paid with a state TR, so he figured it was state business. So, what's going on here?"

"I wish I knew. I really wish I knew. Thanks so much; you've been a great help," Elmer said.

Elmer called an acquaintance at Dutch Harbor that he knew would be privy to all that was going on.

"Yes," the man said, "he was here, but not for long. There was a fellow here, apparently waiting for him. Actually, he looked like an officer of the law—you know the type. Cold and efficient. They left together."

NORTON SOUND

KUSKOKWIM RIVER

BETHEL

ANCHORAGE

BRISTOL BAY

DILLINGHAM

KODIAK IS.

DUTCH HARBOR

"Were they on a regular flight to Anchorage?" Elmer asked.

"I guess I don't know the answer to that." The acquaintance paused. "On second thought, he did mention to Oblensky he'd be traveling with another man. His name sounded like Letkof, or Metkof or something."

Elmer smiled and hung up the phone. He turned to Mary Louise. "Well, it looks like Oblensky has gone too far. Even his son has turned against him, and possibly turned him in."

"What about the note, Elmer? Remember the note Tom found? Couldn't you find out what that meant?"

Elmer sighed and smiled at her. "It seems quite inconsequential now," he said. "But I'll try. I guess my best bet is to call Tom and see if he learned anything about the fellow—perhaps from the captain. He knew Captain Vincent's folks." He turned back to the phone, and called Wardleigh's number.

Elmer smiled at the sound of Tom's voice, so familiar on a multitude of television shows.

"Oh, yes," Tom replied to the question. "He doesn't live here; he lives in Seward. I thought that whole thing was resolved," he said.

"The incident of the girl's death was, but it triggered some ques-

135

tion about the possible illegal sale of bycatch, which might involve his grandfather," Elmer explained.

"Hey, I'm not keen on getting entangled in some business that doesn't involve me," Tom protested.

"I'm not keen on it, myself, but one thing has led to another, and I don't believe the young man is part of it. In fact, I'm quite sure he is not."

"Then why involve him?" Tom asked.

"Only to inquire about what the girl meant in the message on the note," Elmer explained.

"Oh; well, he lives in Seward. He's in the phone book. I'd rather you didn't mention the note. I didn't see that it was addressed to R. Oblensky until I was leaving on the 'copter," Tom said.

"I'll have to mention it, but I don't have to say who found it or what happened to it," Elmer reassured Tom.

The next day, Elmer and his son Ed flew to Seward. They arrived just in time for lunch and went first to a restaurant they knew well.

136

The waitress was a pleasant woman, friendly and chatty. She immediately brought menus and poured coffee.

"Do you know a young man named Oblensky?" Elmer asked.

"Of course," she said. "In a small town like this you know everyone."

"Do you know if he is in town, or out in the Bering Sea?" Elmer added.

"I sure do," she laughed. "He was here just a minute ago. Left his hat over there. He'll be back soon."

They had time to place their order before the young Russian burst into the room and headed for the place where he'd left his hat.

The waitress rushed over to him, nodding toward Elmer and Ed as she talked. He walked over to their table.

Elmer was amazed to see before him a slender young man who smiled as he asked, "You wanted to see me?"

He did not fit the preconceived idea of a seagoing fellow with Viktor Oblensky as his grandfather. Elmer stood up, taking the young man's hand in greeting, as did Ed. "Elmer Rasmuson here, and my son Ed," Elmer said.

"I wanted to see you because I know your grandfather. I'm involved in fisheries management. He seems to have a strong opinion about the observer program, especially the women involved. I thought you might be able to explain that to me," Elmer said.

The young man's expression had changed to one of blank caution. "I have to say, I rarely agree with him. What is it you wanted to know?"

"During the investigation," Elmer said, "they found a note. It was addressed to R. Oblensky, and it read, 'I can't bear it any longer,' or words to that effect. Do you have any idea what that meant?"

"My name is Richard. I am R. Oblensky, to whom she wrote the note." Richard shook his head. Deep sorrow registered on his face. "We were good friends. I wished that we could have been more than that. She was so dedicated to her job. Her reference to me was for me to tell my grandfather to stop bugging her to overlook some of the bycatch figures. He isn't really a crook. He came out of the Russian Revolution and wants to feed the world. Regulations don't mean anything to him. She was going to quit being an observer because of him." He paused, "and I wish she had," he choked out, dropping his head to hide his grief.

Elmer looked at Ed. Ed nodded, as if reading his mind. "End it."

Elmer stood up and touched Richard's shoulder. "We're sorry to have caused you pain. You have been most helpful. Your grandfather must be very proud of you," Elmer said.

Richard turned away to leave, then turned back, his emotions under control. "I know who you are, and appreciate what you have done for good fisheries management. I'm sorry that my grandfather is such a pain in the neck." Then he walked swiftly across the room and out the door.

"Whew," Ed said, "that was heavy. What a fine fellow he appears to be."

Their food came, but they just picked at it before leaving to fly back to Anchorage.

When Elmer arrived at his house there was a phone message from Lee Alverson. "Oblensky arrested for illegal sale of fish," it read.

After Elmer had given Mary Louise a full report of the trip to Seward, he phoned Lee.

"It isn't clear to me why he would be arrested if he was involved with some international agreement about selling over the side," Lee said.

"I dare say he has violated some very strict codes involved. That isn't too difficult to imagine," Elmer replied.

"I suspect our meeting at the Sanno may have been a factor," Lee suggested.

"I dare say. He surely is guilty," Elmer said, "but one would wish that the whole story would be told—not just the story of the pawn."

Addenda

The international North Pacific Fishery Commission reports that the joint venture bycatch figures reached 5,685,714.98 pounds by 1988. In 1989, that figure dropped to 1,926,837.88 pounds. Soon after, the U.S. fleet had grown to proportions capable of harvesting the TAC, and joint ventures ended. However, bycatch remains a rapidly growing problem, with deep-sea trawling the major concern.

The International North Pacific Fisheries Commission, as it was before the Magnuson Act, became nonexistent.

The bycatch problem of the deep-sea trawl fleet becomes one of national interest in 1996.

In 1988, Elmer Rasmuson would receive the Order of the Sacred Treasure from the emperor of Japan for his contribution to the development and preservation of the fisheries of the North Pacific.

After serving on INPFC as chairman, and then on the North Pacific Fishery Management Council as chairman, Elmer's concern for resource management did not retire. He would establish the Rasmuson Fisheries Institute in conjunction with the University of Alaska's School of Fisheries. His goal was to not only support biological research, but to increase study and awareness of the economic and social aspect of the fisheries.

Jim Branson and Clem Tillion were among those members on the Board of Directors of the Rasmuson Fisheries Institute.

★

In 1992, Harold Lokken would receive from the emperor of Japan the Order of the Sacred Treasure for his contribution to development and preservation of the fisheries of the North Pacific. Harold would establish and chair the Pacific Fisheries Foundation in Seattle.

Lee Alverson's son, Robert, would take over Harold Lokken's role as manager of the Seattle Boat Owner's Association.

★

Bob Thorstenson continued to manage Icicle Seafoods until health reasons forced him to retire, but his mind never leaves the concerns of the company. However, his illness does not preclude his able assistance in the development of a series of videos relative to the history of the various fisheries of the North Pacific.

★

Dr. Lee Alverson continues to be negotiator and/or advisor to Canada, and to the U.S. Fisheries and foreign fisheries, as well.

Dr. Alverson's NRC (Natural Resources Consultant, Inc.) 1996 global fisheries report spells out national and international concerns in a most succinct manner.

★

In 1990, Clem Tillion would become Governor Walter J. Hickel's "fish czar" with the governor's main thrust on a community development quota (CDQ) system for the villages along the Bering Sea coast.

★

In 1994, Clem would receive from the emperor of Japan the Order of the Sacred Treasure for his role in the development and preservation of the fisheries of the North Pacific. This award, rarely given to a foreign individual, speaks most clearly of Elmer, Harold, and Clem's contribution to the management of the fisheries of the North Pacific.

★

Gordon Jensen, after twenty years of service, would step down from the Alaska State Board of Fisheries. He would continue to attend meetings pertaining to the industry.

★

Jim Branson would retire as executive director of the North Pacific Fishery Management Council to then become a member of the Board of Directors of APIDCA, one of the CDQ programs, in the Aleutian Islands.

Jim would marry Betty Irvine in 1986.

Tom Wardleigh would become a TV star, teaching Alaskans about flying.

EACH MAN'S
LIFE A
DIFFERENT
ROLE

EACH MAN
WITH A
COMMON
GOAL

TO SEE
THE GAME
FAIRLY
PLAYED

TO SEE
THE FISH
THE WINNER
MADE.

A TESTIMONY TO THEIR CONCERN FOR THE MANAGEMENT OF THE
RESOURCES OF THE SEA.

Elmer Rasmuson

Personal History:

Born February 15, 1909, Yakutat, Alaska
Married to Lile V. Bernard, 1939 (deceased April 1960)
Children: Edward, Lile, and Judy
Married to Colonel Mary Louise Milligan, November, 1961

Education:

Public schools, Alaska
University of Grenoble, France
Degrees—B.S., Magna Cum Laude, Harvard University, 1930
M.A., Harvard University, 1935
LL D (honorary), University of Alaska, 1970
LL D (honorary), Alaska Pacific University, 1993

Professional:

Certified Public Accountant, Alaska, New York, Texas

Business:

Chief accountant, National Investors Corp., NYC, 1933–35
Principle, Arthur Anderson & Co., NYC, 1935–43
President, National Bank of Alaska, 1943–65; Chairman of the Board,
   1966–74; Chairman, Executive Committee, 1975–82; Chairman,
   Budget and Planning Committee, 1982–89; Director Emeritus,
   Chairman

Memberships:

Alaska Bankers' Association (Past President)
American Association for the Advancement of Science
Anchorage Chamber of Commerce (Past Director)
Arctic Institute of North America
Bohemian Club
Defense Orientation Conference Association
Elks Lodge
Explorers Club
Boone & Crockett Club
Eldorado Country Club
Marrakesh Country Club
Thunderbird Country Club
Grand Slam Club
Masonic Lodge
National Association for the Advancement of Colored People
Navy League of the United States (life member) (Freedom Award)
Phi Beta Kappa
Pioneers of Alaska
The Atlantic Council of the United States (Sponsor)
Rotary Club (Past President)
Association of the United States Army
Seattle Yacht Club
West Vancouver Yacht Club
Juneau Yacht Club
Ketchikan Yacht Club

Civic and Public Service:

Member, New York Young Republican Club (officer and Board of Governors) 1933–40
Trustee, Kings Lake Camp, Inc. (Past President) 1944
Director, Anchorage Chamber of Commerce, 1944–46
Member, Anchorage City Council, 1945
Chairman, Anchorage Fur Rendezvous, 1946
President, Anchorage Republican Club, 1947
Secretary, Republican Territorial Convention, Sitka, 1948
Member, Board of Regents, University of Alaska, 1950–69 (President of the Board, 1956–69)
Chairman, Anchorage City Planning Commission, 1950–53
President, Alaska Council Boy Scouts of America, 1953 (Member, Regional and National Councils), Silver Beaver and Silver Antelope Awards)
Delegate, Republican Territorial Convention, Juneau, 1956
Swedish Consul for Alaska 1955–1977 (Knight, Order of Vasa) (Commander, Order of the Northern Star)
Member, Organization Committee of Alaska Methodist University
Civilian Aide to Secretary of the Army, 1959–67 (Outstanding Civilian Service Medal)
Rhodes Scholar Committee, 1960–67 (Past Secretary)
Member, Western Host Committee, International Economic Conference, 1961, 65, 69 & 73
Member, National Advisory Board of Girl Scouts, 1961–67
Chairman, National Security Seminar of Armed Forces, 1963
Member, Governor's Reconstruction Committee, 1964
Mayor, City of Anchorage: Oct. 12, 1964–Oct. 12, 1967
Republican Candidate from Alaska for U.S. Senate, 1968
Commissioner, International North Pacific Fisheries Commission, 1969–84; (Chairman, International Committee, 1971, 74, 77, 80; Chairman U.S. Section 1973–83)
Member, Advisory Committee, Institute of Arctic Biology
Member, Advisory Council on Japan-U.S. Economic Relations, 1971–72
Member, Army and Alaska Command Advisory Boards
Chairman, Rasmuson Foundation
Secretary-Treasurer, Loussac Foundation
Director, Coast Guard Academy Foundation, 1969–84
Member, Joint Committee on United States-Japan Cultural and Educational Cooperation, 1972–73

Member, Marine Fisheries Advisory Committee, 1974–77

Member, Pacific Basin Economic Council, U.S. Executive Committee, 1974–76

Alaska State Chamber of Commerce "Man of the Year," 1974

Alaskan of the Year Award, 1976

Director, Federal National Mortgage Association, 1976

Member, North Pacific Fisheries Management Council, 1976–77 (Chairman)

American Academy of Achievement Gold Plate Award

Member, Board of Directors, Lincoln Institute of Land Policy, 1980–85

Member, Board of Overseers' Committee on University Resources (Harvard), 1980–86

Member, Board of Overseers' College Visiting Committee (Harvard)

Chairman, Alaska Permanent Fund Corporation, 1980–82

Member, U.S. Arctic Research Commission, 1985–92

Dr. Lee Alverson

Education:

B.S. Fisheries, University of Washington, 1950
Ph.D., Fisheries, University of Washington, 1967

Experience:

1943–1946, U.S. Navy, Intelligence Unit
1950–1952, Biologist, Exploratory Fishing and Gear Research Base, Bureau of Commercial Fisheries
1953–1958, Biologist, Washington State Department of Fisheries, Seattle
1958–1968, Lecturer, College of Fisheries, University of Washington, Seattle
1958–1969, Director, Exploratory Fishing and Gear Research Base, Bureau of Commercial Fisheries, Seattle
1969–1970, Associate Director for Fisheries, Bureau of Commercial Fisheries, Washington, D.C. (also served as Acting Director)

147

1969–1976, Affiliate Professor, College of Fisheries, University of Washington, Seattle

1970–1971, Associate Regional Director for Resource Programs, Bureau of Commercial Fisheries, Seattle

1971–1979, Director, Northwest and Alaska Fisheries Center, National Marine Fisheries Service, Seattle

1976–1979, Affiliate Professor, College of Fisheries and Institute for Marine Studies and Program for Social Management of Technology, University of Washington, Seattle

1979–1980, Visiting Professor, part-time, College of Fisheries and 1979–1980, Special Assistant to the Assistant Administrator for Fisheries, National Marine Fisheries Service, Seattle, Institute of Marine Studies, University of Washington, Seattle

1980, Professor without tenure, School of Fisheries and Institute of Marine Studies, College of Ocean and Fishery Sciences, University of Washington, Seattle

1980–1994, Owner/President, Natural Resource Consultants, Inc./Seattle

1995, Owner/Chairman of the Board, Natural Resources Consultants, Inc., Seattle

Overseas Experience:

Fisheries management and development review in Kenya and Tanzania

Project Director, fisheries development in Somalia

Advisor to the Prime Minister on fisheries in the Cook Islands

Chairman, Consultant Group reviewing need for a Maritime College in Oman for the Minister of Education

Chairman, Advisory Committee on Marine Resources Research (ACMRR) on the United Nations Food and Agriculture Organization (UN/FAO)

Member, Board of Trustees, International Center for Living Aquatic Resources Management (ICLARM)

Special Advisor to the Minister of Fisheries, Canada

Special Assignments and Activities:

Advisor to the U.S. Department of State during the negotiations on the International North Pacific Fisheries Commission Treaty

International expert on groundfish to I.N.P.F.C.

148

Fisheries advisor to U.S. Dept. of State on effects of change of breadth of territorial sea

Advisor to U.S. Dept. of State on U.S./U.S.S.R. fisheries problems

1971, Delegate representing NOAA at Law of the Sea Conference

1969–70, Advisor to National Science Foundation on Ocean Decade

Advisor to Governor of Samoa on fisheries development and management

Representative of NMFS at meetings of Deep Ocean Mining Environmental Study (DOMES)

Member, U.S. Delegation to U.S./Japan Consultation on Bristol Bay Salmon and North American Chinook Salmon Conservation Measures

Member, President's Federal Task Force on Washington State Fisheries

Chairman, Advisory Committee on Marine Sources Research (ACMRR) of the United Nations Food and Agricultural Organization (FAO)

Member, Marine Board of the National Advisory of Science

Chief of Staff, U.S. Delegation, U.S/Canada Salmon Interception Negotiations, U.S. Department of State

Member, Fisheries Panel, National Advisory Committee on Oceans and Atmosphere (NACOA)

Member, Washington Sea Grant Steering Committee

Member, Alaska Fisheries Center Study Group by appointment of the Governor of Alaska

Fishing industry negotiator for Marine Mammal Protection Act (MMPA)

Commissioner, U.S. Section, International North Pacific Fisheries Commission (INPFC)

Member, Stellar Sea Lion Recovery Team

Member, Board of Trustees, International Center for Living Aquatic Resources Management (ICLARM)

Advisor to Minister of Education, Oman

Special Advisor to the Minister of Fisheries, Canada

Member, National Academy of Sciences, Oceans Studies Board, Committee on Fisheries and Committee on Bering Sea Ecosystems

Member, National Academy of Engineering, Committee on Review of NOAA's Fleet Replacement and Modernization Plan

Publications:

Author or co-author of over 100 scientific and technical articles ranging in subject matter from opportunities for development of new U.S. fisheries to theoretical considerations in modeling of fish populations.

Honors and Awards:

Phi Sigma Biological Society
Sigma Xi (Full Member, science honorary)
American Institute of Fisheries Research Biologists
Who's Who in the West and American Men of Science
H.R. MacMillan Lectureship, University of British Columbia
Outstanding Civil Service Employee Award
Bureau of Commercial Fisheries Outstanding Scientific Publication
    Award
U.S. Department of Interior Distinguished Service Award for Scientific Achievement
NOAA Award for Scientific Research and Achievement
Golden Halibut Award
First Annual Award, Pacific Rim Alliance of Marine Technology Society
NOAA Unit Citation
U.S. Department of Commerce Gold Medal
Highliner Award
Sport Fishing Institute Commendation
Seiners Association Man of the Year

Harold Lokken

Manager:

Fishing Vessel Owner's Association 1924–1976
International Pacific Halibut Commission:
Conference Board, 1930–1976

Delegate:

U.S. Fishing International Employees/Labor, Geneva, 1950

Negotiator:

International North Pacific Treaty with Japan, 1951
International North Pacific Fisheries Commission
United States Advisor, 1953–1979, Commissioner, 1980

Delegate:

United States, Law of the Sea, Geneva, 1960
U.S. State Department Oceans Affairs:
Commissioner, 1965–1980
Presidential Appointment, National Panel:
Sea Grant Program, 1970–1975
Presidential Appointment:
National Advisory Committee on Oceans & Atmosphere, 1974–1979

Director:

Pacific Fisheries Foundation, 1977–1984

Awards:

Man of the Year, Northwest Fisheries Association, 1963, 1981 Presidential award, Promoting Conservation and Wise use of Natural Resources, 1981 Emperor of Japan: The Order of the Sacred Treasure Gold and Silver Star 1992 Japanese Citation: 1988, Order of the Sacred Treasure Gold and Silver Star

Manager
   Fishing Vessel Owner's Association 1924–1976
   International Pacific Halibut Commission:
   Conference Board, 1930–1976
   Delegate:
   U.S. Fishing International Employees/Labor, Geneva, 1950
   Negotiator:
   International North Pacific Treaty with Japan, 1951
   International North Pacific Fisheries Commission:
   United States Advisor, 1953–1979, Commissioner, 1980
   Delegate:
   United States, Law of the Sea, Geneva, 1960
   U.S. State Department Oceans Affairs:
   Commissioner, 1965–1980
   Presidential Appointment, National Panel:
   Sea Grant Program, 1970–1975
   Presidential Appointment:
   National Advisory Committee on Oceans & Atmosphere,
   1974–1979
   Director:
   Pacific Fisheries Foundation, 1977–1984

Awards:

Man of the Year, Northwest Fisheries Association, 1963, 1981

Presidential award, Promoting Conservation and Wise use of Natural
Resources, 1981

Emperor of Japan: The Order of the Sacred Treasure Gold and Silver
Star 1992

Clem Tillion

Republican Party:

1958: Precinct Delegate
1962: Elected to State House of Representatives
1964: Re-elected to State House

International North Pacific Fisheries Commission:

1966: Appointed to Advisory panel; Chairman, 12 years
1966: Re-elected to State House
1968: One of two Alaska Representatives in negotiations between Japan and the U.S. regarding the Bartlett Bill that extended jurisdiction from three to twelve miles
1968: Re-elected to State House
1968: One of two negotiators with Japan on Bartlett Bill
1969: Advisory to the U.S. State Department on Fisheries, a role that lasted twenty years with numerous trips to Japan, Korea, Russia, Norway, Scotland, and Taiwan
1970–1974: Presidential appointment to NACOA (National Advisory

Committee on Oceans and Atmosphere) during which the Magnuson Act was passed extending jurisdiction to 200 miles

1970: Re-elected to the State House

1972: Re-elected to the State House

1972: Appointment to MAFAC (Marine Affairs and Fisheries Committee) for NOAA (National Oceanic and Atmospheric Administration)

1973: Appointed to vacancy in State Senate

1974: Elected to the State Senate

1976: North Pacific Fisheries Management Council: Charter member

1978–1980: President of the State Senate

1979–1983: Chairman of North Pacific Fisheries Management Council

1982: Presidential Appointment: Alternate Commissioner to the International Fur Seal Commission

1982–1984: Alaska State Director of International Fisheries and External Affairs

1984: International North Pacific Fisheries Commission: Presidential appointment as Commissioner

1990–1994: Special Assistant on Fisheries to Gov. Hickel

1994: North Pacific Fisheries Management Council, Federal appointment (3 year term)

Awards

Wallace H. Noerenberg Award for Fisheries Excellence: American Society, Alaska Chapter

Highliner, Lifetime Achievement Award: National Fisherman

Plaque of Appreciation: Korea Deep Sea Fisheries Association

Bristol Bay Fisheries Corporation: In recognition of support of people in Bristol Bay with the CDQ fisheries issues

Northwest and Alaska Fisheries Center: In recognition and appreciation of your many years of friendship and support

Certificate of Appreciation: United States Department of State certificate of appreciation for advancing foreign policy goals and objectives of the United States pertaining to the living resources of the North Pacific

1994: The Order of the Sacred Treasure Gold & Silver Star: Emperor of Japan

Bob Thorstenson

1949, Graduated, Blaine High School; Fished reef net boat
1950, Western Washington College, fished "Comet"
1951, U.S. Navy, Mine Warfare School (Yorktown)
1952, U.S. Navy Academy Prep School
1953, NROTC Scholarship, University of Washington, Fished Taslum
1954, University of Washington, skipper on "Bernice" (Kayler Dahl)
1955, University of Washington, Varsity crew; skipper "Re Salie" Whiz Fish
1956, Graduated U of W, degree in education, history, Crew Captain, Olympic trials
1957, Fished on power scow "Patty J," S.E. Alaska
1958, Assistant Superintendent, King Cove, P.A.F.
1959, Assistant Superintendent, Petersburg, P.A.F.
1960–62, Superintendent, Petersburg, P.A.F.
1963, General Supervisor, P.A.F. and Vice President of production
1963, Married Pamela Martens

1965–1991, Superintendent of Petersburg Fisheries (Icicle Seafoods)
1967, President, Petersburg Chamber of Commerce
1968–75, Petersburg Chamber of Commerce and School Board
1973–75, MAFAC, U.S. State Dept. Ocean Affairs Committee
1975–86, International North Pacific Fisheries Commission
1976, Director, Alaska State Chamber of Commerce
1978, Alaska Law of the Sea Committee
1981–91, Chairman of the Board, Icicle Seafoods
1991, Retired

Gordon Jensen

Born:

July 19, 1918, Vancouver, B.C.
School, 1–12, Petersburg
Fished halibut fifty years, 1936–1986
Built first boat, "Symphony," 1947
Alaska State Fish and Game Board, 1961–1981
International North Pacific Fisheries Commission Advisory panel,
    1962–1992
Built second boat "Westerly," 1965
International Halibut Commission, 1983
North Pacific Fisheries Management Council, 1977–1980
President, Petersburg Vessel Owners, 1989–1995
International Halibut Commission Conference Board, 1945–1995

Tom Wardleigh

Narration: Tom Wardleigh retired from FAA after twenty-four years with that agency. Tom's memories of flying FAA administrators in Alaska provide a wealth of knowledge concerning how the aviation industry has evolved and changed, and in some cases, why.

Many of today's aviation systems are the result of Tom's contributions. He is regularly consulted by researchers and testers that are in need of expertise. Tom also assists the legal profession with expert witness testimony or as a consultant.

He had originally intended to become a dentist but he came into aviation quite naturally. His childhood memories include the fact that his grandmother bought airplanes, his uncles flew them and also worked in the development of the industry for many years.

Tom's first aviation job came as an apprentice and eventual journeyman mechanic in the propeller division of Pan American Airlines in Seattle in the early forties. After a two-year stint with the U.S. Navy as an aviation machinist mate during WW II, he returned to the Pacific

Northwest to employment with Kenmore Air Harbor at Kenmore, Washington. For five years he was aviation mechanic, shop foreman, and flight and ground instructor.

In 1951 he came to Alaska to work for the U.S. Fish and Wildlife Service as supervisor of fleet maintenance and chief pilot. Tom's experience in the field of resource piloting is probably the most demanding and exciting piloting of his life. He literally wore Grumman Widgeons, and Gooses for days-on-end during the summer seasons.

The places he flew and landed aircraft to get a job done were incredibly intricate and demanding at times.

The Grumman Gooses that are still flown by the Department of Interior and the State of Alaska were all acquired by Tom as surplus aircraft from the Navy between the years 1952 to 1955. Not only did he acquire them, he flew them to Alaska, filled to capacity with spare parts.

In 1959, Tom was hired away from the Fish and Wildlife Service to the Federal Aviation Administration by Jack Jefford, a widely renowned Alaska pilot and FAA pilot.

Jack Jefford had preceded Tom in both agencies.

Tom has in excess of thirty thousand hours of flight time in everything from the smallest of aircraft through large multi-engine and small jets such as Sabreliners, Gulfstreams, and Citations.

Tom continues to instruct several hundred hours per year and is much in demand, particularly for advanced ratings and both single and multi-engines Sea-ratings.

In recent years he accrued hours flying an "AG truck," hauling everything from baby fish to fertilizer to fuel.

Tom's industry associates are innumerable and worldwide. He has participated at OshKosh, as an instructor, presented safety programs around the country for government agency pilots, both state and federal. He has served as Chairman of the Board of the Alaska Aviation Safety Foundation since 1984, bringing the Foundation recognition as a positive influence in the field of aviation safety with FAA, AOPA, OPOA Safety Foundation, EAA, 99's and Industry researchers.

Every hour Tom flies is exciting to him whether it is with a brand new student or in a corporate King Air.

His personal goal is to give as much information and expertise to the industry as he feels has been given to him over the years.

He tirelessly pursues that goal.

Brad Matsen

My father was a soldier, my mother was a nurse. They grew up, as I did, near Bridgeport, Connecticut, although the Army moved us around the world during the middle years of my childhood. I graduated from high school at Fort Bragg, North Carolina, went to the University of North Carolina at Chapel Hill for a couple years, then, in 1963, fled the then-tedious and confusing business of a traditional education for the far more engaging lessons of Southeast Alaska.

I had a friend whose father worked in the Forest Service there and he let us pitch our tent in his backyard while my friend and I looked for work. As usual, Fish and Game was hiring stream guards, so we took the job everybody told us was a one way ticket to misery in the bush with a chance of getting shot by creek robbers. Though we had one tense encounter with a seiner, the season was an idyll of camping, camp food, astounding scenery, fear of bears which were everywhere around our Admiralty Island cover. It also marked my transformation from boy to man.

161

A year later, with the Vietnam war at all ahead full, I ran ahead of the draft into the U.S. Marine Corps to attend flight school in Pensacola, Florida. After basic flight, rheumatic fever laid me low and after six months in the hospital, I washed out of Advanced Flight and transferred to the National Security Agency. Just married to Colleen Simpson, who I'd met in Juneau, and with four more years to go on my Marine Corps hitch, I took an assignment to the Monterey Language Institute in California. There, I studied Russian for a full year, then went to San Angelo, Texas, and Fort Devans, Massachusetts, for cryptanalytic training and finished my tour in the Corps at a clandestine listening post in Scotland. I also worked for the agency as a linguist and analyst in Norway, Crete, Germany, and England before returning to the U.S. for discharge in 1970.

Finishing a degree was never more important to me, so I returned to college and a year later had a BA in English Literature, had published several short stories, and decided to try for a life as a writer. I returned to Alaska, went to work for the state ferry system on deck, unsuccessfully, to weave the week on-week off schedule into my writing life. I also built myself and my wife a house on a wilderness peninsula north of Juneau and conceived my daughter, who would become Laara Estelle Matsen. A streak of good fortune then sent me to the University of California in Newport Beach where I became a University Fellow and candidate for a Master of Fine Arts in fiction. I finished the degree in 1975, finished a novel that was never published, and returned to Alaska once again. Back on the ferries as a deckhand and steward, I quickly decided that the schedule was hard on a family and looked for other work, since writing was clearly not paying the bills. I was publishing stories, but for very little money.

Another streak of good luck brought Jay Hammond into the Governor's Mansion and gave a lot of people my age a good reason to serve the state by working for him. I became a special assistant to the Commissioner of Health and Social Services, Dr. F.S.L. Williamson, who asked me to represent him in a variety of capacities.

In 1977, my wife and I divorced and left the state and I resigned from public service to become a fisherman. I bought a small troller and, for two years, enjoyed the wildly free life of trolling for salmon in the most beautiful waters in the world. After my second season, in 1979, I realized that my daughter was growing up in my absence, so I left Alaska to live near her and her mother in Seattle. I returned to writing, working on the script and book for the film "Spirit of the Wind" and also became a freelance contributor to the *Alaska Fisherman's Journal,* a publication for the commercial fleets. Six months after filing my first story, I was in the editor's chair at the *Journal,* where I remained for five years.

The exhilaration of covering the post-Magnuson Act fisheries off Alaska was, to that time, the most valuable experience of my life. I had complete access to fishermen and managers and a distinguished forum in which to publish my work. Nothing could be better, and in 1985, when I was forty, I moved on to become the Pacific Editor at the nation's premier fishing magazine, *National Fisherman.*

My heart and the central friendships of my life remained in the commercial fishing community, and I realized that there and in Alaska, I had found the home that had eluded me most of my life. My home territory is now really a migratory range from Monterey Bay, California, to Kachemak Bay, Alaska, arguably two of the most dramatic and resonant patches of water on the Pacific, and I am at home anywhere in between. Commercial fisherman continue to evolve through the collisions of the human population explosion and the tender fish stocks on which we depend for food and for our vision of ourselves as adventurous, productive people. I suppose I'll continue to evolve with them.

Professional Credentials

Academic:

Bachelor of Arts, 1972, University of North Carolina, Chapel Hill
Master of Fine Arts, 1975, University of California, Irvine

1966–1970, U.S. Marine Corps, Charter pilot; Commercial Fisherman; Merchant seaman
1970–present, Writer and photographer; Books, Essays, Documentary Films, Magazine articles, Exhibits, and Advertising
1975–1978, Editor, *Alaska Health Quarterly*
1978–1979, Publisher and Editor, *Film Seattle,* a monthly cinema guide
1980–1984, Editor, *Alaska Fisherman 's Journal*
1982–1984, Associate Editor, *Seafood Leader Magazine*
1985–present, Senior Editor, *National Fisherman Magazine,* and *Seafood Business Magazine*

Jim Branson

1946–1948, Fished salmon and albacore off the coast of Washington
and California

1949–1951, Enforcement Officer for U.S. Fish and Wildlife Service,
Southeast Alaska

1952, U.S. Fish and Wildlife Service, Anchorage

1953–1955, U.S. Fish and Wildlife Service Agent-in-Charge; Kenai
and Kodiak Districts

1956–1957, U.S. Fish and Wildlife Service Agent-in-Charge, Kenai
District

1958–1962, U.S. Fish and Wildlife Service Supervisory, Anchorage
District

1963–1976, National Marine Fisheries Service Agent, Kodiak and
Aleutian Island District

1977–1988, Executive Director, North Pacific Fisheries Commission

FIRST THERE
WERE THREE.

THEN THERE
WERE MORE.

THEN CAME
THE TIME

TO CLOSE
THE DOOR.

"NO, NO",
THEY CRIED

"LET US
PLAY, TOO"

"WE'VE BOUGHT
THE CHIPS,

WE KNOW
THE RULES."

AT

THE GREAT NORTH PACIFIC CASINO

Data

50 lb. halibut produces 500,000 eggs
250 lb. halibut produces 4,000,000 eggs
Developing ova found at 300 to 1500 feet
Largest halibut on record 9 feet long weighing 700 lbs.

TAC = Total allowable catch
CEY = Constant exploitation yield
MSY = Maximum sustainable yield
ASP = Annual surplus production
MFCMA = Magnuson Fisheries and Conservation Act
IPHC = International Pacific Halibut Commission
INPFC = International North Pacific Fisheries Commission
HANA = Halibut Association of North America
PICES = Pacific International Commission re Exploration of the Seas
ICES = International Council for the Exploration of the Seas

If you're coming in for a landing and you're behind the power curve, you cannot put on enough power to save yourself . . . Jim Thurston.

1888

Completion of the Northern Pacific Railroad made it possible to ship product to the East coast where stocks were depleted. Schooners headed for the North Pacific around the Horn.

First vessels were the halibut schooner *Oscar & Hattie*, the sealing vessel *Edward E. Webster*, and the halibut schooner, *Mollie Adams*.

Norwegians had depleted the North Sea. They sailed to the east coast of the North Atlantic. They, plus the Canadians, and the American fishermen of the North Atlantic depleted those stocks, then came around to the North Pacific.

166

Ocean Forum (Jackson & Royce)
p. 42 . . . Alaskan cod grounds—450 metric tons by 1868 (salted) then fluctuated from 200 to 1200 MT until 1890.
p. 46 . . . Salmon canneries or saltries all the way North to Bristol Bay—in 1882, 30,000 metric tons.

Politics and Conservation (Cooley)
p. 71 . . . In the 1880s the U.S. Fish Commission began scientific investigations in Alaska. During the ensuing years, as commercial exploitation increased, the Secretary of the Treasury frequently suggested to Congress that the Fish Commission should take over the Federal responsibility of fishery management in Alaska; but the Fish Commission resisted the move. It conceived its role as one of pure scientific research.

1890

1975 Report

Establishment of East Coast Co.'s cold storage to provide ice and cold storage for shipment (steam vessels).
New England Fish Company operated winter and summer

1892

Pioneering a Modern Small Business (Blackford)
p. 3 . . . Japanese started taking king crab in the Sea of Japan

1894

Politics and Conservation (Cooley)
p. 28 . . Alaska Packers Association of San Francisco owned or controlled 90% of salmon canneries in Alaska

1894

1975 Report
Still fishing out of dories
Ocean Forum (Jackson & Royce)
p. 46 . . . salmon production: 60,000 metric tons

1896

Icicle . . . Boca de Quadra Inlet, "Quadra Packing" salmon
(Buschmann)
Ocean Forum (Jackson & Royce)
. . . an Act restricting the use of nets in rivers for salmon but with little
provision for enforcement.

1898

Icicle . . . Petersburg Packing; Buschmann-salmon

1899

1975 Report . . . Icy Straight Packing. Salmon packer at Petersburg
built wharf and provided glacier ice.
Sailing schooners, 20–40 tons
Steam powered, 50,000–100,000 tons
Both using Gloucester dories. Two men per dory pulling three or four
1800' skates of gear a day.

1900

Ocean Forum (Jackson & Royce)
p. 47 . . . Salmon hatcheries were primary method of conservation; re-
leasing 200–600 million fry. Laws applicable to Alaska required
companies taking sockeye salmon to operate a hatchery producing
four times as many as the adult fish captured.

1901

Icicle . . . Chatham Straights Packing-Buschmann
Ocean Forum (Jackson & Royce)
p. 46 . . . salmon production, 150,000 metric tons

1902

1975 Report . . . San Juan Packing Co. established first freezing plant
   at Taku Harbor, (first in Alaska)
(Icicle) . . . Buschmann sold to Pacific and Navigation

1903

Icicle . . . Alaska Packers Association who owned 70% of Alaska's
   salmon pack dropped the price of pink salmon and broke PPNC
   (Buschmann destroyed, died)

1904

Thompson . . . West Coast production, 20 million pounds, five times
   that of the East coast

Conservation and Politics (Cooley)
p. 77 . . . Dr. Jordon called attention to the appalling condition of the
   fishery and the inadequacy of the existing conservation measures.

1905

Icicle . . . "Pacific Coast of Norway" closed cannery at Tonka and took
   over and built a larger "Petersburg Incorporated."

Ocean Forum (Jackson & Royce)
p. 42 . . . Cod increased to 5,500 metric tons

1906

Politics and Conservation (Cooley)
p. 78 . . . A comprehensive Alaska Fisheries Conservation Bill was introduced in the House of Representatives. The Bill provided for the extension of authority to cover all fishing to the three-mile limit (U.S. jurisdiction), provide an Alaska Fishery Fund for scientific studies and tax rebate for the development of hatcheries.
p. 82 . . . The Act as passed bore little resemblance to the original comprehension . . . etc.

The Act of 1906 provided ample testimony to the growing political strength of the canned salmon industry.

1907

Fish for Tomorrow (Gilbert)
p. 22 . . . "meetings which never accomplished any results as to the purported objective of maintaining the resource because the discussions always resolved themselves down to a division of the spoils."

1908

Fish for Tomorrow (Gilbert)
p. 22 . . . The Treaty of 1908; consisting of Dr. David Starr Jordan from the United States and Prof. E.E. Pruice of Canada—to investigate the fisheries shared by the two countries.

1910

Thompson
1910–1920 increased efficiency—the Cape Flattery, British Columbia, and South East Alaska grounds were seriously depleted. Halibut spawned from mid-December to mid-May.
Fish for Tomorrow (Gilbert)
p. 44 . . . The introduction of gasoline engines as auxiliary to sail. The ability to improve icing facilities set the stage for a break out by the fleet beyond Cape Ommany to Coronation Island and beyond.

1911

Pacific Halibut (Bell)
p. 71 . . . Average halibut take (all area total) = 64,330,000 pounds

Politics and Conservation (Cooley)
The governor of Alaska, Walter E. Clark, appealed to President Taft to influence Congress to pass a law protecting the salmon fisheries, which he said were seriously injured for lack of proper safe guards.

1912

Pacific Halibut (Bell)
p. 71 . . . average halibut take (all area total) = 64,330,000 pounds

1913

Pacific Halibut (Bell)
p. 71 . . . average halibut take (all area total) = 64,330,000 pounds

1914

Pacific Halibut (Bell)
p. 71 . . . average halibut take (all area total) = 64,330,000 pounds

Fish for Tomorrow (Gilbert)
p. 23 . . . Canada, disgusted by delays in results of the Treaty of 1908 withdrew from the Treaty.

Politics and Conservation (Cooley)
p. 92 . . . The governor of Alaska pointed out in his annual report that conservation had been applied to nearly every resource of Alaska save the fishery.

1915

Pacific Halibut (Bell)
p. 71 . . . average halibut catch (all area total) = 64,330,000 pounds

Icicle . . . Petersburg Packing Co. bought 50% of the stock in Petersburg and took over.

1916

Thompson . . . tried seasonal closure versus year around fishing due to 70% depletion per decade. Average take of halibut, 44,900,000 pounds.

Pacific Halibut (Bell)
p. 233 . . . Month of May, 3 million pounds of halibut were taken from an area known as "the lightship grounds," literally cleaned out in a few months. On Sept. 16 a vessel chartered to the Fish Commission caught four fish.

Politics & Conservation (Cooley)
p. 93 . . . Governor of Alaska, John Strong, made a direct attack on the Bureau of Fisheries and its politics.

1917

Icicle . . . Petersburg Packing Co. gained 100% control.

Pacific Halibut (Bell)
p. 71 . . . Average halibut take, 44.9 million pounds (total all areas)

1918

Pacific Halibut (Bell)
p. 71 . . . average halibut take (all areas), 44.9 million pounds.

Fish for Tomorrow (Gilbert)
p. 31 . . . The second International Sockeye Commission . . . and in the

fall "for all the comprehension manifest in this problem the Treaty drawn by the International Commission of 1918 reveals a degree of political ineptitude which was amazing in politicians and of which the Commission was primarily composed."

1919

Pacific Halibut (Bell)
p. 71 . . . average annual landings (all areas), 44.9 million pounds

Fish for Tomorrow (Gilbert)
p. 48 . . . The first Halibut Treaty: Its purpose was the conservation of a fishery shared by the United States and Canada. The abortive attempt to include such extraneous and controversial subjects as port facilities and tariffs in a treaty conceived for the conservation of a shared ocean fishery doomed the document to failure.

Politics and Conservation (Cooley)
p. 28 . . . The Federal Trade Commission reported the five canning companies (salmon) controlled over 53% of the pack.

1920

Pacific Halibut (Bell)
p. 71 . . . average annual landing (all areas), 44.9 million pounds

Pioneering a Modern Small Business (Blackford)
p. 3 . . . Japanese expanded king crab to the Bering Sea with floating canneries. Americans entered king crab fishery at Seldovia; Arctic Packing Co. which was joined by Alaska Year Around cannery (small effort).

Fish for Tomorrow (Gilbert)
p. 35 . . . Effective attacks doomed the Treaty of 1918, but it rested in the Senate.

1921

Pacific Halibut (Bell)
p. 71 . . . average total halibut landings, 50.1 million pounds

1923

Ocean Forum (Jackson & Royce)
p. 27 . . . The Halibut Treaty of 1923. International Fisheries Commission provided for research on halibut and limited regulatory authority precipitated by declining stocks.

1924

Pacific Halibut (Bell)
p. 71 . . . average total halibut landings, 50.1 million pounds.

Ocean Forum (Jackson & Royce)
. . . "White Act" governed the Fed's role on salmon in Alaska. It required 50% escapement. The scientists studies were basically on the life of the salmon, not on regulation (U. of W. Fisheries Institute).

IPHC #22
p. 34 . . . The Halibut Commission went into effect on exchange of ratification on Oct. 23. It provided a three month closed season during the reg.'s for halibut caught out of season.

Conservation and Politics (Cooley)
p. 124 . . . The "White Act" passed—"no exclusive right of fishery, nor shall any citizen be denied the right to take, prepare, cure, or preserve fish or shellfish in any areas of the waters of Alaska where fishing is permitted . . . that not less than 50% of the salmon run should be allowed to spawn."

1925

Pacific Halibut (Bell)
p. 71 . . . average total halibut landings, 50.1 million pounds.

Politics and Conservation (Cooley)
p. 132 . . . an International Pacific Salmon Conference was held (Washington, Oregon, California, and Canada). It brought out that although scientific study had been going on for nearly half a century the actual knowledge of salmon was lamentably small . . . "if we tried to conduct agriculture on the basis of such ignorance anyone would think we were daft." . . . they established the "International Pacific Salmon Investigation Federation."

1926

Pacific Halibut (Bell)
p. 71 . . . average total halibut landings, 53.6 million pounds

1927

Pacific Halibut (Bell)
p. 71 . . . average total halibut landings, 53.6 million pounds

1928

Pacific Halibut (Bell)
p. 71 . . . average total halibut landings, 53.6 million pounds

Thorstenson . . . Petersburg cold storage with glacier ice

Pioneering a Modern Small Business (Blackford)
p. 3 . . . Russians entered Bering Sea for king crab

Politics and Conservation (Cooley)
p. 130 . . . Skinner and Eddy purchased Alaska Consolidated Canneries. E.B. Deming, president of Pacific American Fisheries Co. purchased 12% of the entire American pack of salmon.

p. 131 . . . a feeling of complacency was generated at the top level in D.C. by the continual praise and assurance received from the industry. Total production continued to increase. The Bureau seemed wholly unable to make an independent decision and carry it through.

1929

Icicle Seafoods, Thorstenson
Pacific American Fisheries gained control of Petersburg Packing Co.
The first delegate from Petersburg to the Halibut Association.

Pacific Halibut (Bell)
p. 71 . . . average total halibut landings, 53.6 million pounds

1930

Ocean Forum (Jackson & Royce)
p. 26 . . . Japanese crab canning mother ships with catcher boats in Bering Sea.
p. 27 . . . New authority for IFC providing halibut research and limited regulatory authority.
p. 42 . . . Japanese start trawling for cod, flounder, halibut, and other fish.
p. 48 . . . Canada and U.S. negotiated the "Sockeye Salmon Fisheries Convention" but not ratified until 1937 re U.S. groups opposing establishing a commission for scientific investigations of the decline of the Fraser River salmon run . . . after eight years came to conclusion was rock slide at Hell's Gate.

Pacific Halibut (Bell)
p. 71 . . . average total halibut landings, 53.6 million pounds

1931

Pacific Halibut (Bell)
p. 71 . . . average total halibut landings, 46.1 million pounds

IPHC #22 . . . "Conference Board," Advisory Panel designated by union and vessel owners organizations (halibut).

1932

Pacific Halibut (Bell)
p. 71 . . . average total halibut landings, 46.1 million pounds

1933

Pacific Halibut (Bell)
p. 71 . . . average total halibut landings, 46.1 million pounds

Pioneering a Modern Small Business (Blackford)
p. 3 . . . American imports of king crab from Japan, 7 million pounds a year.

Politics and Conservation (Cooley)
p. 135–36 . . . The Association of Pacific Fisheries passed a resolution calling for closer collaboration with Northwest Salmon Canner's Association and the Pacific Canned Salmon Brokers Association to bring unity of purpose in dealing with the urgent problems . . . committees formed to handle labor problems . . . representatives in Washington D.C. . . . . Territorial relations, etc.
Thorstenson . . . Petersburg Packing became a P.A.F. cannery

1935

Ocean Forum (Jackson & Royce)
p. 16 . . . that Japan was fishing salmon outside three miles in Bristol Bay was first made public.

Pacific Halibut (Bell)
p. 71 . . . average halibut total landings, 46.1 million pounds

177

1936

Pacific Halibut (Bell)

p. 71 . . . average halibut total landings, 51.2 million pounds

Ocean Forum (Jackson & Royce)

p. 25 . . . salmon pack peaked at 300,000 metric tons. Japan dispatched
a trawler type vessel of 657 tons.

p. 26 . . . and two other vessels to investigate the salmon and other fisheries of Bristol Bay.

Thorstenson . . . Gordon Jensen started long lining for halibut in the
"Teddy J."

Politics and Conservation (Cooley)

p. 35 . . . The peak for the entire period was reached of commercial exploitation (of salmon) when a total of 8.5 million cases were
packed.

p. 141 . . . Testifying before House and Senate Fisheries Committee
against a Bill introduced to close down (salmon) traps in Alaska.
Edward W. Allen directed the canner's testimony. One of the key
witnesses was J.M. Gilbert representing Alaska Pacific Salmon
Co. He opposed the Bill on grounds it was confiscatory, that it defeated the ends of conservation . . . he concluded . . . "I think instead of decreasing catch it will be possible to increase it as runs
build up. I think the Bureau of Commercial Fisheries can and may
possibly say for the benefit of this hearing that commercial fishing
has tended to increase the runs by reason of the fact that over-
escapement in certain streams will almost annihilate the runs . . .
in other words, over-escapement has been proven to be much
worse than over-catch of fish, and the Bureau of Fisheries can support that statement I am sure."

The testimony of A.W. Brindle, president of Ward Cove Canning Co.
amplified Gilbert's.

p. 143 . . . Delegate Anthony J. Dimond presented the main testimony
in favor of the Bill. "The principle purpose to help keep a fair part
of the very enormous wealth in the Territory where it was created
. . . the room is all but filled with operators who pack on a big scale,
but they have carefully refrained from making any statement to
the committee . . . it is well to remember that the small packers
have little stake in this measure as compared with the great corpo-

rations who dominate the salmon packing industry of Alaska."
The only decision was to study the situation.

1937

Pacific Halibut (Bell)
p. 71 . . . average total halibut landings, 51.2 million pounds

Ocean Forum (Jackson & Royce)
p. 26 . . . Pacific Fisherman carried articles of "Alien Invasion," that
brought about the "Sockeye Salmon Fisheries Convention." Sea-
faring nations supported the three-mile limit concept.
U.S. herring production 114,000 metric tons
p. 27 . . . third version of IFC negotiated

IPHC #22
North Pacific Halibut Act, limiting bringing halibut caught in convention waters only to those vessels in nations part of the convention.

1938

Pacific Halibut (Bell)
p. 71 . . . average total halibut landings, 51.2 million pounds; Japan
produced 18% of the world's total fish production, 3,780,000 metric
tons.

Pioneering a Modern Small Business (Blackford)
p. 5 . . . Lowell Wakefield and Sons were operating a herring reduction
plant at Port Wakefield on Raspberry Island, Kodiak, Alaska.
Icicle . . . Brindle leased PAF as "Petersburg Co."

Politics and Conservation (Cooley)
p. 149 . . . Bureau of Fisheries was transferred from Commerce to Interior.

1940

Pacific Halibut (Bell)
p. 71 . . . average total halibut landings, 51.2 million pounds

Icicle . . . Brindle leased PAF as "Petersburg Co."

Politics and Conservation (Cooley)
p. 149 . . . Bureau of Fisheries merged with the Bureau of Biological
Survey, an agency for the preservation of wildlife, to the Fish and
Wildlife Service.

1941

Pacific Halibut (Bell)
p. 71 . . . average total halibut landings, 53.0 million pounds

Pioneering a Modern Small Business (Blackford)
p. 4 . . . Congress appropriated funds for survey of Alaska's fisheries resources, king crab and other fish than salmon.

1942

Pacific Halibut (Bell)
p. 71 . . . average total halibut landings, 53.0 million pounds

1943

Pacific Halibut (Bell)
p. 71 . . . average total halibut landings, 53.0 million pounds

1944

Pacific Halibut (Bell)
p. 71 . . . average total halibut landings, 53.0 million pounds

Pioneering a Modern Small Business (Blackford)

p. 35 . . . Nick Bez convinced the War Food Administration the Bering Sea was rich in protein and they supplied him with a 6,000-ton freighter *Mormarcy* to use as a floating cannery and freezer mother ship and four 100-foot trawlers (RFC financed) supplied the ship. The *Mormarcy* was re-named the *Pacific Explorer*. The adventure did not get going until after the war. (Pacific Exploration Co.)

1945

Pacific Halibut (Bell)

p. 71 . . . average total halibut landings, 53.0 million pounds

Concern for the fishery of the Japanese increase in fishing the North Pacific increased with the ending of the war when the already increasing capability was developing to feed the people of Japan.

Thorstenson . . . Gordon Jensen had his own boat *Symphony* 57'. A highliner fishing the Gulf of Alaska.

Pioneering a Small Modern Business (Blackford)

p. 6–7 . . . Beginnings of Wakefield's deep sea trawlers (for king crab). (Attracted to this because he felt herring was almost fished out and halibut and salmon over-crowded.)

1946

Pacific Halibut (Bell)

p. 71 . . . average total halibut landings, 57.3 million pounds

Ocean Forum (Jackson & Royce)

p. 26 . . . first major (U.S.) crab fishery in the Bering Sea

p. 27 . . . in Northwest Europe, the Over Fishing Convention, to draw on results of world research on fisheries since 1902 by the International Council for the Exploration of the Seas. (ICES)

p. 67 . . . salmon production dropped to 150,000 metric tons (canned product)—(from the peak of 300,000 metric tons in 1936)

p. 21 . . . Japanese production from the sea, 2,000,000 metric tons

p. 24 . . . Pacific Fisheries Conference urging Truman Proclamation

Thorstenson . . . Gordon Jensen, "I attended the Deep Sea Fisherman's Union of Seattle and then the Petersburg Vessels Owners, so I represented both groups. We met in Harold Lokken's office. When he asked, 'Who represents the vessel owners?' I said, 'I did,' and when he asked, 'Who represents the Union?' I said, 'I did.'

1947

Pacific Halibut (Bell)
p. 71 . . . average total halibut landings, 57.3 million pounds

Pioneering a Small Modern Business (Blackford)
p. 168 . . . king crab production (Bering Sea and Alaska) U.S. 250,000 pounds (Wakefield 170,000)

Ocean Forum (Jackson & Royce)
p. 24 . . . establishment of the University of Washington Fisheries Research Institute. The main purpose to research salmon. The salmon industry in Alaska was the most valuable fishery in the U.S.
Second Pacific Fisheries Conference urging Truman Proclamation after Dept. of State announced "suspended progress."
Bristol Bay fishermen want power. Terrible storm drowns over 100 fishermen, helpless without it.

1948

Pacific Halibut (Bell)
p. 71 . . . average total halibut landings, 57.3 million pounds

Ocean Forum (Jackson & Royce)
p. 24 . . . Dr. Wilbert Chapman appointed Special Advisor on Fisheries to the Undersecretary of State (then Director of the College of Fisheries, U. of W.).
SCAP (Supreme Commander for the Allied Powers) excluded Japan from the Eastern Bering Sea.
p. 21 . . . Japan's production from the sea, 2,518,000 metric tons
p. 26 . . . Canada's herring production, 200,000 metric tons

Pioneering a Small Modern Business (Blackford)
p. 36 . . . "Pacific Explorer" began work in earnest with twelve chartered catcher boats catching more than could be processed canned 430,000 pounds. (Nick Bez, Pacific Exploration Co.)
p. 17 . . . By Nov. the "Deep Sea" was a collapsed operation.
Squeaky Anderson sends gill net boats up Cook Inlet to test fishery potential.

1949

Pacific Halibut (Bell)
p. 71 . . . average total halibut landings, 57.3 million pounds

Ocean Forum (Jackson & Royce)
p. 24 . . . The USSR was using vessels fitted out by the U.S. Lend Lease arrangements and building more vessels for the North Pacific. A fishery mission to Japan headed by Edward Allen of Seattle, Frederick Bundy of Glouster, Maine, and Donald Loker of Terminal Island, California. (Fisheries of the Northwest, New England ground fish, and California tuna, respectively.) The thrust of the mission was to press for an enlarged fishery scientific organization in Japan—pressed for the elevation of the fisheries agency.

Politics and Conservation (Cooley)
p. 42 . . . 154 salmon canneries (in Alaska)

Pioneering a Small Modern Business (Blackford)
p. 18 . . . Deep Sea Trawlers taken over by Apex (Wakefield's father's company) and found crab in April.
Canneries hire watchmen with guns. Gillnet fishermen rob traps.

1950

Pacific Halibut (Bell)
p. 71 . . . average total halibut landings, 57.3 million pounds

Pioneering a Modern Small Business (Blackford)
p. 168 . . . king crab production, Bering Sea and Alaska 600,000 pounds (Wakefield 420,000)

Ocean Forum (Jackson & Royce)
p. 14 . . . salmon declined to half the 1936 peak
Japanese annual catch = 3,374,700 metric tons
Japan was taking 17% of world catch, U.S. 12%

Thorstenson . . . Gordon Jensen also starts to seine for salmon as well
   as fish for halibut. Delivers once to Seldovia.
Ownership and Productivity of a Marine Resource (E. Keene).
p. 38 . . . fishers had invested a least eight or nine times more capital in
   vessels and gear than was necessary to harvest halibut in area A
   and possibly four times in area B.
Gillnet fishermen sweep into Cook Inlet from Kodiak and South East.
Squeaky Anderson has only halibut delivery station north of Kodiak.

1951

Pacific Halibut (Bell)
p. 71 . . . average halibut total landings, 62.0 million pounds

Thorstenson . . . of the 147 canneries started, 59 remained; concern
   over decline of stocks. 1951 pack = 1,115,175 cases. Average had
   been 1,679,056 cases. (difference of 563,881 cases)

Ocean Forum (Jackson & Royce)
. . . The International Convention for the High Seas Fisheries of the
   North Pacific Ocean was negotiated. A tripartite convention of Japan, Canada, and the U. S. with abstention as a new International
   concept. Stocks included halibut off coasts of Canada and U.S., exclusive of the Bering Sea and waters west of the tip of the Alaska
   Peninsula and salmon off the coast of Canada and the U.S., exclusive of the Bering Sea and waters of the North Pacific west of 175
   w longitude.

1952

Pacific Halibut (Bell)
p. 71 . . . average total halibut landings, 62.0 million pounds

Pioneering a Modern Small Business (Blackford)
p. 168 . . . king crab production, Bering Sea and Alaska = for Japan
1,400,000#s, U.S. 934,000#s, (Wakefield 550,000)

1953

Halibut season, 52 days, May 17–July 12

Ocean Forum (Jackson & Royce)
p. 122 . . . The International Convention for the High Seas Fishery of
the North Pacific Ocean came into force June 12, 1953. It under-
took to "ensure the maximum sustainable yield of the resources of
the North Pacific Ocean and established a Commission (INPFC)
the International North Pacific Fisheries Commission."
p. 27 . . . (IFC) was re-named as the International Pacific Halibut Commission. (IPHC) . . . Canada and the U.S.
p. 28 . . . Overseas Convention of 1946 was ratified.
Japanese resume king crab fishery, eastern Bering Sea.

Pot fishing for king crab starts in Kachemak Bay
Kodiak Mirror reports "Jim Branson, U.S. Fish and Wildlife agent (in
PBY) catches illegal halibut boat off Aleutians."
Old timers accuse Clem of "spoiling everything," when he starts fishing
in winter

1954

Halibut season = 68 days, May 16–July 12

Pacific Halibut (Bell)
p. 71 . . . average total halibut landings, 62.0 million pounds
. . . Japanese resume groundfish trawling in Eastern Bering Sea
Clem fishes halibut and king crab and gill nets for salmon. Friend Paul
Becker sends info from Armed Services Institute re fisheries of the
North Pacific and Maragawa's 30-year study on king crab. USFW
pilot Tom Wardleigh stops by with biologists to talk fish. Wake-
field trawlers, with pots aboard as well, move into Kachemak Bay.
Processors Dick Haltiner and Squeaky Anderson oppose. Distant

water fleet explodes. Japanese, Polish, British, Russians, Spanish, and Bulgarians in Gulf of Alaska and Bering Sea.

1955

Halibut season = 93 days, May 12–August 4

Pacific Halibut (Bell)
p. 71 . . . average total halibut landings, 62.0 million pounds

Politics and Conservation (Cooley)
p. 67 . . . salmon production dropped to below 100,000 metric tons.

Pioneering Modern Small Business (Blackford)
p. 1 . . . Squeaky Anderson testifies (at fishery meeting about king crab) "I'm testifying for the female king crab," he said. "Yes, I get thrown back overboard when they lift the trawl but my legs are broken or missing, my shell is loose from my body. I may or may not survive. Crab pots are kinder to me."
p. 70 . . . (cannery man): "I know of no practical way to tie a boat to us except through the use of money . . . but in each case it takes from ten to fifty thousand dollars."
p. 80 . . . Wakefield produced 1,240,000 pounds (king crab total industry was 1,830,000)

1956

Halibut season, 105 days. May 12–August 24

Pacific Halibut (Bell)
p. 71 . . . average total halibut landing, 67.7 million pounds

Ocean Forum (Jackson & Royce)
p. 107 . . . The USSR never signed a peace treaty with Japan and objected to them fishing the high seas; especially off the Kamchatka Pen. which precipitated the Convention Concerning the High Seas Fishery of the North Pacific.
Canada suggested prohibition of net fishery for salmon on high seas off North America. Feds and State had to agree. It failed.

... Clem starts Narrows Packing Co., processing shrimp
... People talking statehood
... Clem likes idea of a Commonwealth
... Branson likes it like it is
... Main issue, fish traps owned by outside interests
... Volunteer lay-up plan for halibut, supported by eighteen organizations

Pioneering a Modern Small Business (Blackford)
p. 141 ... Dr. Norman Wilimovsky also reported that signs of serious depletion were apparent in Kachemak Bay.

1957

Halibut season, 144 days, May 1–Sept. 22

Pacific Halibut (Bell)
p. 71 ... average total halibut landings, 67.7 million pounds

Ocean Forum (Jackson & Royce)
p. 107 ... U.S. moved to recommend cessation of Japanese fishing during the 1958 season in areas west of the line.
... Narrows processed 23,000 pounds of shrimp; stopped when Seattle company canceled 20 ton order. Partner quit, Norman Nilson sells 10 tons held in cold storage but, defeated and deeply in debt Clem takes a charter for the king crab research program and assist in building the Kasitsna Bay Lab. Tags crab all winter.

1958

Halibut season, 119 days, May 4–August 31

p. 71 ... average total halibut landings, 67.7 million pounds (U.S. = 40.4 million pounds)
King crab production U.S. total 4,660,000 pounds (Wakefield 2,180,000), Soviets, 702,000 and Japan, 1,700,000 pounds.

Ocean Forum (Jackson & Royce)
Alaska Statehood. William Egan, Governor
. . . Japanese began whaling along Aleutian Islands
. . . Soviets began whaling near the Aleutians, king crab and ground-
fish trawling in the eastern Bering Sea.

Pioneering a Modern Small Business (Blackford)
p. 1 . . . By the late fifties Americans, Canadians, Japanese, and Russians were competing for resources. Wakefield expands.
p. 141 . . . King crab catch fell off alarmingly despite an intensification
of fishing effort.
p. 142 . . . Alaskan companies urged that trawling be totally banned,
that pot limits be imposed upon most waters and that a licensing
scheme be put into effect to prevent vessels from moving from one
fishing area to another during a single season.

Politics and Conservation (Cooley)
p. 35 . . . the last year of Federal management and control, the total
(salmon) pack amounted to only 1.6 million cases; over five times
lower than 1936.
p. 42 . . . fifty-one canneries operating (less than in 1910)
p. 52–53 . . . early in the century there were approximately 3,000 fishermen in the industry while in the late 50s there were well over
12,000.
p. 67 . . . Dr. James Crutchfield of the University of Washington drew
the following conclusion regarding Alaska salmon, "until, and unless it becomes possible to reduce the amount of gear to the minimum needed to take the permitted catch, economic waste,
widespread violation of regulations, and a threat to the very existence of the industry will remain."

1959

Swanson River Oil strike

1960

Halibut season, 85 days, May 1–July 25

Pacific Halibut (Bell)
p. 71 ... average total halibut landings, 67.7 million pounds (U.S. halibut catch = 38 million pounds)

Pioneering a Modern Small Business (Blackford)
Japan produced 4,130,000 pounds of king crab.

1961

Halibut season, 105 days, May 10–August 23

Pacific Halibut (Bell)
p. 71 ... average halibut landings, 67.9 million pounds (U. S. catch = 40 million pounds)
Japanese began shrimp fishing, central Bering Sea
Halibut Association of North America

Pioneering a Modern Small Business (Blackford)
p. 143 ... Alaska Department of Fish & Game banned trawling in all state waters and extended area licensing to Prince William Sound.
King crab production; processed pounds (Japan = 4,130,000) (Soviet Union = 2,500,000) (U.S. = 8,878,000/Wakefield was 3,000,000)

1962

Halibut season, 94 days, May 9–August 11

Pacific Halibut (Bell)
p. 71 ... average total halibut landings, 67.9 million pounds (U.S. catch = 40.2 million)

Ocean Forum (Jackson & Royce)
p. 102 ... INPFC organized a Gulf of Alaska Ground fish Committee, separate from the Biology and Research Committee.
INPFC agreed to remove abstention from halibut fishery in the Bering Sea. (re U.N. Law of the Sea) The Convention on the Territorial Sea and Contiguous Zone (not more than 12 miles).
The Convention on the High Seas established principles of internationally relating to the high seas.

IPHC#22 . . . removed the 175 degree west longitude abstention line

Pioneering a Modern Small Business (Blackford)
p. 84 . . . Japan produced 5,640,000 processed pounds of king crab.

1963

Halibut season, 92 days, May 9–August 9

Pacific Halibut (Bell)
p. 71 . . . average total halibut landings, 67.9 million pounds (U.S. halibut catch = 34.1 million pounds)
Salmon season reduced to 4 days a week
King crab production in processed pounds (Japan = 5,640,000) (Soviet Union = ?) (U.S. = 18,200,000/Wakefield = 6,400,000)

Ocean Forum (Jackson & Royce)
p. 123 . . . Japanese began long line fishing in the central Bering Sea re negotiations of INPFC (intense emotions, but it's re-negotiated).
Japan starts fishing halibut in the Bering Sea . . . called "The Bering Sea Give Away."
Rampart Dam big issue in Legislature
Oil spills in Cook Inlet . . . "acts of God" . . . by defenders of oil companies
Heavy fines imposed (God became not so careless)

Pioneering a Modern Small Business (Blackford)
p. 101 . . . the value of Alaska's king crab pack surpassed halibut.
Wakefield produced 6,413,000 pounds of crab.

1964

Halibut season, 110 days, May 1–August 19

Pacific Halibut (Bell)
p. 71 . . . average total halibut landings, 67.9 million pounds (U.S. catch = 26.2 million pounds).

Icicle . . . PAF sold many of its canneries

Ocean Forum (Jackson & Royce)
p. 128 . . . Soviets began shrimping in the Gulf of Alaska
Because of decline in halibut Japan volunteered to cease participation
    in quota fishery
At the invitation of the Governor of Alaska, Japan sent ships to buy
    salmon after U.S. companies and fishermen could not settle on a
    price.
p. 146 . . . re Law of the Sea . . . "The Convention on the Continental
    Shelf." This provided that the coastal state had unshared conser-
    vation authority over the living resources of the high seas adjacent
    to its Territorial Sea; if the conservation measures were based on
    appropriate scientific findings and did not discriminate against
    foreign fishermen.(!)
Oil companies interests were involved

Earthquake . . . Special Session . . . Borough Bill
Area licensing issue

Pioneering a Modern Small Business (Blackford)
p. 105 . . . Japanese dispatched 700 vessels . . . bottomfish, salmon, and
    crab, with a subsequent pack of 5,640,000 pounds
Soviet Union sent 400 vessels
p. 106 . . . dramatic increase in U.S. competition
p. 144 . . . Alaska Department of Fish & Game reversed its earlier
    stand and abolished pot limits.

1965

Pacific Halibut (Bell)
p. 71 . . . average total halibut landings, 67.9 million pounds (U.S. hali-
    but catch = 30.2 million pounds)
. . . king crab production, processed pounds (Japan = 4,400,000) (Soviet
    Union = 2,846,000) (U.S. = 31,609,000/Wakefield = 8,200,000).

Icicle ... PAF sold cannery to "Petersburg Fisheries," organized by its
    bookkeeper, Bob Thorstenson, and fishermen, Gordon Jensen,
    Magnus Martens, and Thomas Thompson. Of Bob, they said, "He
    isn't dancing up a storm now, he's sweating over getting the money
    together."

Ocean Forum (Jackson & Royce)

p. 112–13 . . . Unrest against Japan reached peak but return was 54 million while Japan took 7 million. INPFC forced to address conflict of fisheries organizations in both countries. Clarence Pautzke made eloquent speech against high seas gill net fleet.

p. 26 . . . Japanese invest. Elmer Rasmuson meets with Lokken and Alverson and company managers.

Pioneering a Modern Small Business (Blackford)

p. 101 . . . Wakefield produces 8,200,000 pounds of crab.

p. 136 . . . established Quality Control Board. 1% landing tax for funding.

1966

Pacific Halibut (Bell)

p. 71 . . . average total halibut landing 56.0 million pounds (U.S. halibut catch = 30.1 million pounds)

King crab production in processed pounds (Japan = 4,400,000) (Soviet Union = 2,846,000) (U.S. = 40,372,000/Wakefield = 7,100,000).

Pioneering a Modern Small Business (Blackford)

Preface . . . King crab production peaked at 160,000,000 pounds

p. 99 . . . Wakefield starts construction of Seldovia plant

p. 105 . . . Pan Alaska's crab and bottom fish output = 5,470,000#s

p. 136 . . . The QCB hired Herb Hilscher to lobby.

Ocean Forum (Jackson & Royce)

Japanese salmon fish; Chukchi Sea

Soviets trawl for Pacific hake off Washington & Oregon

Thorstenson . . . Gordon Jensen had the *Westerly* built. 72', 11" wide, steel, after the experience of having a comber roll over the stern . . . "I just stood there," he said, "watching the boat disappear and wonder if she'd come back up. I figured I'd used up all my luck."

. . . Hickel runs for Governor.

Clem is appointed to INPFC Advisory Committee. (Harold Lokken one of the four U.S. Commissioners)

Re-up of the bilateral with Japan

1967

Pacific Halibut (Bell)
p. 71 . . . average total halibut landings, 56.0 million pounds (U.S. halibut catch = 29.7 million pounds)

Ocean Forum (Jackson & Royce)
p. 147 . . . the committee on the Sea Bed by the U.N. (25 groups of issues and hundreds of meetings held to draft procedures and articles)

IPHC#22
p. 37 . . . Japan stops fishing halibut in the Bering Sea

Decline in halibut prices (7 million dollar loss) 80% attributed to misuse of name "Greenland halibut," resulting in legal change in '68 to "Greenland turbot."
Re-up bilateral with Japan—USSR extended

1968

Halibut season, 164 days, May 4–Oct. 15

Pacific Halibut (Bell)
p. 71 . . . average total halibut landings = 56.0 million pounds (U.S. catch = 19.2 million pounds)

Ocean Forum (Jackson & Royce)
p. 168 . . . world production from wild stocks tripled from 1950 to 1970
Governor Hickel sends Clem and Jay Hammond to Japan, re 12 mile limit extension (Bartlett Bill). Clem studies Japanese.

Prudhoe Bay oil fields come in.

Pioneering a Modern Small Business (Blackford)
p. 120 . . . Unexpected industry-wide over production dropped prices and then a scarcity of crab.
p. 126 . . . Wakefield merged with Hunt-Wesson

1969

Halibut season, 138 days

Pacific Halibut (Bell)
p. 71 . . . average total halibut landings = 56.0 million pounds (U.S. catch = 24.8 million pounds)
King crab production in processed pounds (no Japanese or Russian figures) (U.S. = 12,823,000/Wakefield = 2,500,000)
Bartlett Bill (12 mile extension of jurisdiction)
Truman Doctrine . . . control of Continental Shelf
Japanese given quotas of halibut in the Bering Sea. The U.S. fleet did not fish.
Bad feelings result
28% decrease in halibut since 1960 (19% Canadian)

1970

Halibut season, 149 days, April 25–Sept. 21

Pacific Halibut (Bell)
p. 21 . . . average total halibut landings, 56.0 million pounds

Icicle . . . Petersburg Fisheries expanded to Seward with "Seward Fisheries."

Ocean Forum (Jackson & Royce)
p. 101 . . . total number of foreign vessels exceeded 500 (*i.e.* large factory trawlers in addition to several hundred vessels engaged in salmon and crab.) Total catch reached 1,850,000 metric tons.

Alaska Department of Fish & Game adopt a quota system for king crab.

1971

Halibut season, 178 days, May 7–Nov. 1

Pacific Halibut (Bell)

p. 71 . . . average total halibut landings, 34.0 million pounds (U.S. catch = 21.2 million pounds)

Koreans (R.O.K.) began pollock fishing in the Bering Sea

1972

Halibut season, 136 days

Pacific Halibut (Bell)
p. 71 . . . average total halibut landings, 34.0 million pounds (U.S. catch = 20.4 million pounds)

Icicle . . . Petersburg Fisheries and Petersburg Cold Storage merge

Ocean Forum (Jackson & Royce)
. . . Japanese began octopus and squid fishery in the Bering Sea, Koreans, sablefish and pollock in the Gulf of Alaska.

. . . Re-up bilateral with Japan
Alaskans voted to amend the "no exclusive right of fishery" in the Constitution

1973

Halibut season, 144 days

Pacific Halibut (Bell)
p. 71 . . . average total halibut landings, 43.0 million pounds (U.S. catch = 17.3 million pounds)

Legislature voted to confirm "no exclusive right of fishery"

1974

Halibut season, 121 days

Pacific Halibut (Bell)

p. 71 . . . average total halibut landings, 34.0 million pounds (U.S. catch = 13.9 million pounds).

Pioneering a Modern Small Business (Blackford)

Ocean Forum (Jackson & Royce)
p. 147 . . . The final sessions of the committee on the Sea Bed by the U.N met in Caracas after hundreds of meetings and convened after ten weeks; disbanding without adoption of any treaty text.

1975

Halibut season, 128 days

p. 71 . . . average total halibut landing, 34.0 million pounds (U.S. catch = 16.3 million pounds)

Ownership and Productivity of Marine Fishery Resources (Keen)
p. 41 . . . between 1973 and 1975 Alaska divided its salmon fishery grounds into 19 areas and instituted separate limited entry programs into each . . . salmon catches in Alaska increased . . . Alaska salmon resources still are subject to far more fishing effort than is needed.

Ocean Forum (Jackson & Royce)
p. 147 . . . Polish begin rockfish fishing; Gulf of Alaska

1976

Halibut season, 96 days
U.S. catch = 15.5 million pounds

Icicle . . . Petersburg Fisheries acquired interest in "Sitka Sound Seafoods" and changed the name to "Icicle Seafoods"

Ocean Forum (Jackson & Royce)
p. 101 . . . foreign fleets; Bering Sea = 1,600,000 (SO) 400,000 MT.
Vessels over 5 net tons fishing halibut numbered 743, vessels smaller, 3,597

p. 148 . . . because of the lengthy negotiations on the "Law of the Sea" issues the U.S. Congress developed interim legislation resulting in the (Magnuson) "Fisheries Conservation and Management Act," and the "200 mile fishery conservation zone."

Pioneering a Modern Small Business (Blackford)
p. 146 . . . the king crab total pack stood at 106 million live weight pounds.

Ownership and Production of Marine Fishery Resources (Keen)
p. 36 . . . because of the quota imposed by the IPHC, the halibut (of the North Pacific) did not go the way of the North Atlantic.

1977

Halibut season, 47 days
U.S. catch = 13.1 million pounds

Icicle . . . Petersburg Fisheries purchased "Alaska Seafoods" at Homer. Changed name to "Icicle Seafoods."

IPHC#22
p. 37 . . . Canada and U.S. extend jurisdiction obviating authority of INPFC relative to halibut.
March 1, President Ford signs "Fisheries Conservation Act" . . . formation of 9 regional Councils around U.S. coast. Clem sits in Gallery of Congress as it passes.
Elmer Rasmuson first Chairman of North Pacific Fisheries Management Council.
Harold Lokken and Clem, members.

1978

Halibut season, 43 days

Ocean Forum (Jackson & Royce)
p. 153 . . . Canada extended to 200 miles
John Negroponte: U.S. State Dept., Bureau of Oceans & International Environmental & Scientific Affairs, with the support of Elmer

Rasmuson, INPFC, moved the fishing line available to Japanese fleet from 175 W to 175 E, to the Asiatic side and with adjusted dates. The Bristol Bay run was not hit by that foreign fishery.

IPHC#16
p. 31 . . . the coast-wide catch of halibut is estimated to be 20,000 fish annually or about 250,000 pounds. The effect of the sport catch on stock abundance is considered to be of minor importance relative to the commercial catch and the incidental catch of halibut by foreign and domestic trawlers.

1979

Halibut season, 32 days

Icicle . . . the "Star" division was formed by Petersburg with two large floating plants operating in western Alaska.

IPHC#22
p. 35 . . . the 1979 protocol to the Halibut Convention of 1953 optimizing production from all parts of area 2 by Canada and the U.S. based on scientific and other sources.

Ownership and Production of Marine Fishery Resources (Keen)
p. 14 . . . a skipper from Oregon discovered that widow rockfish concentrate in mid-water at night in large schools that could be caught with mid-water trawls . . . it became overfished in two years.

1980

Halibut season, 20 days

INPFC 1990
p. 244 . . . incidental halibut catch (foreign = 4,311 metric tons/U.S. joint ventures = 286 metric tons)

Ocean Forum (Jackson & Royce)
p. 156 . . . Japan salmon ranching a large share of the Asian chum salmon market.

Canadians phased out fishing halibut in U.S. waters.

1981

Halibut season, 13 days

INPFC 1990
p. 244 . . . incidental halibut catch (foreign = 2,704 metric tons/U.S. joint ventures = 232 metric tons)
Governor Hammond appoints Clem to be Alaska State Director of International Fisheries and External Affairs

Pacific Halibut (Bell)
p. 99 . . . with no further "war holidays" as yet, the over-all catch of halibut by all nations off Iceland has undergone another dismal decline over the past two decades (representing a 70% decline)
p. 103 . . . there is no reason to believe the Pacific halibut stocks are not as vulnerable . . . if the destruction of young recruits by trawling is not stemmed or stayed promptly the extinction of the Pacific halibut fishery will be more traumatic and more rapid than was experienced by the halibut stocks and fishery off New England.

It cannot be proven beyond all reasonable doubt that trawling for other species of demersal fish has been the prime cause of decline in halibut yields in all parts of the northern oceans, but to disregard the consistency and timing of the circumstantial evidence would border on the irresponsible. To credit the declines to some long term changes in survival of recruitment conditions in all parts of the northern hemisphere but with each part having its own time scale is even more untenable.

1982

Halibut season, 11 days

INPFC 1990
p. 244 . . . incidental halibut catch (foreign = 1,609 metric tons/U.S. joint ventures = 563 metric tons)

Ocean Forum (Jackson & Royce)
p. 147 . . . The Convention (Law of the Sea) was adopted

IPHC#22
p. 36 . . . North Pacific Halibut Act—for regional fisheries management councils who may provide for the rural coastal villages of Alaska the opportunity to establish a commercial halibut fishery in areas of the Bering Sea to the north of 59 N latitude during 3-year development period.

1983

Halibut season, 7 days

INPFC 1990
p. 244 . . . incidental catch of halibut (foreign = 1,872 metric tons/U.S. joint ventures = 438 metric tons)

FAO, (Rome) . . . Consultation on the regulation of fishing effort (fishing mortality) Fernand J. Daucet, "in spite of the fact that none of the quota schemes met all or most imperatives, they all represent an improvement over previous management systems (on the need of a quota system)."

1984

Halibut season, 5 days

INPFC 1990
p. 244 . . . incidental catch of halibut (foreign = 2,128 metric tons/U.S. joint ventures = 617 metric tons)

IPHC#22 estimated incidental catch at 10 million pounds (Is the difference sport fishing? Pot fishery? Other long line?)

Thorstenson . . .Gordon Jensen had an accident, turns boat over to son. "Of course he fishes everything. When Chris took over he fished cod, halibut, black cod, salmon, fall black cod, and king crab." . . .

"I've always disagreed with those guys (State) on seasons; I think they're over-fishing."

Clem appointed Commissioner on INPFC

1985

Halibut season, 4 days

INPFC 1990
p. 244 . . . incidental catch of halibut (foreign = 1,789 metric tons/U.S. joint ventures = 1,026 metric tons)

Ocean Forum (Jackson & Royce)
p. 157 . . . PICES, a scientific organization of members from the U.S., Canada, Japan, Russia, and other Pacific interests pending . . . counterpart to ICES on the Atlantic and may supplant INPFC.

85% increase in landings of halibut in Alaska. . . . Kodiak = 28.5% . . . Prince Rupert, Seward, and Sitka, each = 7.3% . . . Homer = 6.4% . . . Seattle = 5.9% . . . Vancouver = 5.4%, and Petersburg = 3.8%

1986

Halibut season, 4 days

INPFC 1990
p. 244 . . . incidental halibut catch (foreign = 1,192 metric tons/U.S. joint ventures = 1,711 metric tons)

Ocean Forum (Jackson & Royce)
p. 180 . . . The entry of Japan into Alaska salmon processing came with the withdrawal of major U.S. food companies in the fluctuating market.
p. 183 . . . The most promising, in theory, appears to be ownership of a right to fish by each fisherman. This should be transferable, like title to a piece of land and permit the market place to determine who fishes profitably and who sells the right to fish. . . . Not acceptable to most fishermen.

1987

Halibut season, 3 days

INPFC 1990
p. 244 . . . incidental halibut catch (foreign = 1,1077 metric tons/U.S.
joint ventures = 1,485 metric tons)
Foreign fishery ended in Gulf of Alaska

1988

Halibut season, 4 days

INPFC 1990
p. 244 . . . incidental halibut catch (U.S. joint venture = 2,579 metric
tons)

Icicle . . . Petersburg "Star" division added three more vessels.
Foreign fishery ended in Bering Sea.

Ownership and Productivity of Marine Fishery Resources (Keen)
p. 49 . . . full property rights in pastures of the oceans will lead to far
more efficient management of our fisheries resource (means International Government)
p. 51 . . . working with nature means just the work . . . working with nature to produce these things for harvest is seldom considered fun,
requiring capitol and physical labor that in no way connotes the
fun of fishing, hunting, or picking berries.
p. 52 . . . the warped investments made in attempt to compensate for
the controlled aspect of fishing effort under limited entry show
clearly that the imperatives of the commons described above are
not removed.

1989

Halibut season, 4 days

INPFC 1990

p. 244 . . . incidental halibut catch (U.S. joint venture = 875 metric tons)

1990

Halibut season, 3 days

Clem becomes Special Assistant to Governor-elect Walter J. Hickel
Dec., Ottawa, Canada . . . "North Pacific Marine Science Organization" delegates from Canada, China, Japan, Soviet Union, and the United States (PICES)

Honolulu Advisor
Dec. 7 . . . "Don't let it happen here, local fishermen say catches decline but no one really knows whether fishing stocks are harmed by over fishing . . . even the absence of positive proof of a decline in fish stocks should not keep us from applying common sense . . . Hawaii doesn't have to wait for the disasters that befell Mainland fisheries where action was taken too late."

The Star Bulletin, Hawaii
Dec.10 . . . "We have to really fight," he (Inouye) said, adding that he and others are working on legal strategy, "we should be allowed to fish where we want."

1991

Halibut season, 2 days
Incidental catch of halibut = 47,500,000#s

IFQ (individual, transferable quota) issue before the North Pacific Management Council. The Tillion/Hegge plan.

1992

Halibut season, 2 days
Incidental catch

Icicle . . . "Icicle Seafoods" operates a surimi products plant and re-processing plant in Bellingham, Washington, and 50% ownership in canned products warehouse in Astoria, Oregon. The company is owned by its fishermen and employees.
1992 worldwide sale = 230 million dollars.
NMFS, halibut vessels with I.Q.'s = 7,073
Sablefish = 2,168

1993

Halibut season, 1 day
Incidental catch

Icicle . . . (Petersburg Fisheries) bought "Portlock Smoked Salmon."
Gordon Jensen—"The American trawl fleet hit the bottom fishery thinking they were not subject to the restrictions on the foreign fleet. We're doing exactly the same thing as we did 32 years ago."

CDQ Program (Community Development Program for Bering Sea villages) involves 7.5% of total pollock . . . it sold for close to 30 million.

New York Times (David Pitt) . . . "World Fisheries in Peril, U.N. says."

Mary Harwood . . . Unless some form of strict management action is taken, these stocks will be driven further and further down toward levels from which they will not be able to recover.

1995

The first season with the new Individual Quota system in place.
No fisherman drowned in the long line fleet. Many fishermen who had testified against the system had to confess that it was wonderful to go fishing when the weather was tenable or seek a market for their fish for a better price and the public cheered with fresh fish in the market place.

1996

The re-authorization of the Magnuson Act passed Congress as the Magnuson/Stevens Act. Senator Stevens, who had worked with Magnuson for the first, the 200-mile extension, richly deserved to be recognized in the re-authorization by Congress.

Bibliography

Bell, F.H. *Pacific Halibut: The Resource and the Fishery*. Seattle: Alaska Northwest, 1981.

Blackford, Mansel G. *Pioneering a Modern Small Business: Wakefield Seafoods and the Alaskan Frontier*. Ed. Glenn Porter. In *Industrial Development and the Social Fabric,* Series Vol. 6. Greenwich, CT: Jai Press, 1979

Cooley, Richard. *Politics and Conservation.*

Gilbert, John D. *Fish for Tomorrow*. Ed. Marcus Drake, et al. University of Washington School Fisheries Press, 1988.

Honolulu Adviser.

International Pacific Halibut Commission.

Keen, Elmer A. *Ownership and Productivity of Marine Fishery Resources: An Essay on the Resolution of Conflict in the Use of Ocean Pastures*. Tulsa: M&W Publications, 1988.

The New York Times, article by David Harwood and Mary Pitt.

Star Bulletin, Hawaii.

Thompson, Arne. Paper delivered to author.

Thorstenson, Robert, CEO Icicle Seafoods. Statement delivered to company.

Bibliography